AN HEIR AND
FOUR SPARES

The Five Bennet Boys

A semi-original work
by Gretel Hallett

Introduction

I am indebted to Rory Muir for the idea for this interpretation of 'Pride and Prejudice'. In "Gentlemen of Uncertain Fortune, How Younger Sons Made Their Way in Jane Austen's England", he pointed out that the sons of gentlemen in Regency England were not as free to do as they pleased as we might think, and faced limited options when it came to their life choices. There were very few avenues open to those gentlemen's sons who had to earn their own living. And he speculated on what life for the Bennet brothers may have been like; in many ways it would have been very different than for the Bennet sisters; but also, that many surprisingly similar problems would still have occurred.

The eldest son would inherit, where the eldest daughter could not; but there would still be little provision for the younger children in either case. Mr Bennet's estate simply wasn't big enough to support more than one grown-up son's family. In Jane Austen's England, younger sons of gentlemen had surprisingly few choices for making enough money to live upon. Traditionally, the eldest son inherited the father's estate, the second son became a clergyman and the third son went into the army or navy. There were a few office jobs, like that of Mr Philips, the Attorney in Meryton, and some bold souls went to India; but actually, young gentlemen's lives were almost as circumscribed as those of their sisters in what was considered a suitable path forward into adult life. As we can see from Miss Bingley's reaction to Mr Gardiner; trade was not quite respectable enough for a gentleman to pursue. Gently reared young women in Regency England were expected to marry a gentleman with enough money to keep them and their children; but their brothers had to somehow earn their money in order to afford a wife.

At the end of his book, Mr Muir speculates on what the parallel roles might have been for five Bennet sons, in place of the five Bennet daughters in 'Pride and Prejudice'. In his conclusion, he writes, 'The ... masculine counter part of Jane Bennet is obvious. As the eldest he would have inherited the estate when his father died, and if he had been the true equivalent of Jane, he would have provided generously for his mother and been a good and helpful brother to his siblings, much as Edward Knight was for the Austen family. But he would also have married and had a family of his own, and would have expected his younger brothers to make their own way in the world once they were fairly launched.

'If Lydia had been a boy he would surely have joined the army, for 'scarlet fever' infected adolescents of both genders. (...) The fate of the male version of Catherine, the second youngest of the Bennet children, is less clear. He might have followed Lydia's counterpart into the army ... but family tradition has it that Jane Austen imagined Catherine being improved by the marriages of her two eldest sisters ... and ultimately marrying a clergyman ... In our alternative universe, it is possible that he himself became a clergyman ... The career of Mary's counterpart is as obvious as that of Lydia's – he would have become an attorney, being articled to Uncle Philips. Indeed, family tradition again says that Austen indicated that Mary herself would 'obtain nothing higher than one of her Uncle Philip's [sic] clerks'. ... And what of   Elizabeth? What career would her male equivalent pursue? Probably not the army, the navy or India ...'

He goes on to suggest that Elizabeth's male counterpart might be apprenticed to her Uncle Gardiner in London and learn his trade, but goes on to admit, 'Still, it was very unlikely that a young man brought up in the   business by the Gardiners would even make the acquaintance of a Georgiana Darcy, and virtually impossible that he would propose and be accepted.' (pps 321 – 323). In fact, it is hard to imagine what a   masculine version of Lizzie might have done in order to get ahead in life.

This was my starting point, and I renamed the five boys; John, Edward, Mark, Charles and Luke. John would join with Mr Bennet to end the entail on Longbourn – but then what of Mr Collins? He is both no longer a threat, and no longer able to attempt to marry one of them, and throw their mother into a frenzy by marrying Charlotte Lucas instead. And what of John? With no Jane, there is no lustrous marriage to Mr Bingley!

Edward, I decided would follow Edward Knight, and be adopted by a rich distant relative. That, of course, brings problems of its own; namely, that he would not be at Longbourn for the majority of the action, nor would he travel north with Mr and Mrs Gardiner and get caught out at Pemberley. Finally, he would not meet, infuriate, and finally marry Mr Darcy.

Of course, I could, at this point have turned Mr Collins into a homicidal maniac who murdered his way through the Bennet sons in order to inherit Longbourn; and I could have made Darcy and Edward homosexual, so that they could indeed meet, clash, and finally marry. But I shall leave those two plot options for someone else to explore.

Mark, I decided, certainly could become articled to Mr Philips; it's a very neat solution indeed, and suits his pedantic and self-important character. And Charles could, eventually, go to Oxford, and then be awarded a living at Pemberley by Mr Darcy – but clearly there would have to be a strong connection between the two families for that to happen.

And Luke could still be just like Lydia; impetuous, untamed, brash, and obsessed with officers, but because he wanted to BE one, rather than marry one. The problem with turning Lydia into Luke, is Mr Wickham of course. He can still attempt to damage Darcy by nearly eloping with Miss Darcy – but he is less likely to elope with Luke than he was with Lydia; and there would be far less of a scandal about their running away together anyway – young men in Regency England did not have a 'bubble reputation' to be burst in the same way that the young women had.

I started by attempting to plot a story for these new characters, and come up with solutions to the problems named above – and they are not the only ones by any means! What of Lady

Catherine? She cannot attempt to browbeat Edward into not marrying Miss Darcy, and Edward will not be visiting Charlotte at her humble parsonage in Hunsford either, therefore he will not learn the truth about Wickham at that point in the story. It seemed as though I would have to drop Mr Collins, and Lady Catherine all together – and my novel would be very much the poorer for it.

I was getting nowhere very slowly, as well as getting very confused, when I decided to go back to the original novel. What if I simply typed it out, pretty much as it is, but changed the gender and names of the Bennet children? And that is where I really appreciated the sublime genius of Jane Austen far more than I have ever done in four decades of reading her novels. It fitted! It is nowhere near as good as her original, because I am not Jane Austen; she was a genius, I am a plagiarising hack. There has been some shoe-horning going on, and I have had to change some of the characters' motivations, and even some of their relationships to each other – but every time I picked up the book again, there Miss Austen was, providing me with the perfect line for the characters I had poached so blatantly.

The eagle-eyed reader will instantly spot exactly where I have copied out of 'Pride and Prejudice' word for word, as well as where I have had to insert pieces of my own creation, and where I have attributed speech to a different character to Jane Austen's original. They will also see the creaky plot joins, and the very occasional (I hope!) improbability and inconsistency in character and plot.

Like many people, I adore Jane Austen's world, and I have eagerly read as many spin-offs from it as I have been able to find. Some are really very good, and I have made my recommendations at the end of this book, others were simply dire. But there is a thirst to carry on with Austen's wonderful characters and with novels set in her wonderful world; and like many readers, I want to know 'what happened next?' This was an exercise for me in actually finishing a writing project; in immersing myself in Jane Austen's sublime world again, and seeing how different it might look if the five daughters were five sons instead. I have really enjoyed writing this, and I hope you will enjoy reading it, and maybe even mildly approve of how I have affected the changes, and the outcomes they led me to.

And finally, please remember, this is a work of fiction. I did not set out to traduce Jane Austen's sacred memory, nor to imitate her; I simply set out to see what would happen if I answered Mr Muir's question – what would have happened if the Bennet girls had been the Bennet boys?

Chapter One

It is a truth universally acknowledged, that a man in possession of an entailed estate must be in want of a son to join with him to cut off the entail imposed by a suspicious ancestor. This, Mr Bennet gloomily concluded, was all very well and true, but what does a man with a moderate income entailed estate do when his lady presents him with not one, but five sons?

It is another truth universally acknowledged that a single man in possession of a good fortune, must be able to assist those who are not so fortunate, especially younger sons, and it is greatly to his credit if he has sisters with good fortunes who are disposed to marry those younger sons too.

However little known the feelings or views of such a man may be on his first entering a neighbourhood, these truths are so well fixed in the minds of the   surrounding families, that he is considered the rightful benefactor of one or other (hopefully all) of their younger sons.

"My dear Mr Bennet," said his lady to him one day, "have you heard that Netherfield Park is let at last?"

Mr Bennet replied that he had not.

"But it is," returned she, "for Mrs Long has just been here, and she told me all about it."

Mr Bennet made no answer.

"Do not you want to know who has taken it?" cried his wife impatiently.

"You want to tell me, and I have no objection to hearing it."

This was invitation enough.

"Why my dear, you must know, Mrs Long says that Netherfield is taken by a young man of large fortune from the north of England; that he came down on Monday in a chaise and four to see the place, and was so much delighted with it that he agreed with Mr Morris immediately; that he is to take possession before Michaelmas, and some of his servants are to be in the house by the end of next week."

"What is his name?"

"Bingley."

"Is he married or single?"

"Oh! Single, my dear, to be sure! A single man of large fortune, four or five thousand a year. What a fine thing for our boys!"

"How so? How can it affect them?"

"My dear Mr Bennet," replied his wife, "how can you be so tiresome! You must know that he will have livings in his gift, and connexions in the city, the Army or the Navy, and he will have sisters with fortunes of their own for our sons to marry!"

"And is it his design in settling here to assist our sons?"

"Design! Nonsense, how can you talk so? But it is very likely that he will want to help well-deserving young men to get on in the world, and his sisters may fall in love with one of them, and therefore you must visit him as soon as he comes."

"I see no occasion for that. You and boys go, or send them by themselves with a note to say they are all of age, and available for heiresses to marry whenever they wish. And as for Mr Bingley, you are as handsome as any of our boys, and he might like you the best of the party."

"My dear, you flatter me. I certainly have had my share of beauty, but I do not pretend to be anything extraordinary now. When a woman has five grown-up sons to place in the world, she ought to give over thinking of her own beauty."

"In such cases, a woman has not often much beauty to think of."

"But, my dear, you must indeed go and see Mr Bingley when he comes into the neighbourhood."

"It is more than I engage for, I assure you."

"But consider your sons. Only think how it could benefit them. Sir William and Lady Lucas are determined to go, and in general you know they visit no new comers. I suspect they will push Charlotte at Mr Bingley as a wife. Oh, if only we had a daughter, I would be very pleased to see her as mistress of Netherfield, not that encroaching Charlotte Lucas. Indeed, you must go, for it will be impossible for us to visit him if you do not."

"You are over-scrupulous surely. I dare say Mr Bingley will be very glad to see you; and I will send a few lines by you to assure him of my hearty consent to any thing he may feel inclined to do for our sons, although John is not in need of a rich man's assistance, so I will put in a word for Edward in his stead."

"I desire you will do no such thing. Edward is not a bit more deserving than the others, and indeed you know very well that he is taken care of also. At any rate he is not half so handsome as John, nor half so good humoured as Luke. But you are always giving him the preference."

"They have none of them much to recommend them, except John who has been to University and can hold a sensible conversation, but Edward has something more of quickness than his brothers."

"Mr Bennet, how can you abuse your own children in such a way? You take delight in vexing me. You have no compassion on my poor nerves."

"You mistake me my dear. I have a high respect for your nerves. They are my old friends. I have heard you mention them with consideration these twenty years at least."

"Ah! You do not know what I suffer."

"Well, I hope you will get over it and live to see many young men of four thousand a year, multiple

complaisant sisters, and gifts of livings and influence, come into the neighbourhood."

"It will be no use to us, if twenty such should come since you will not visit them."

"Depend upon it, my dear, that when there are twenty, I will visit them all."

Mr Bennet was so odd a mixture of quick parts,   sarcastic humour, reserve and caprice, that the   experience of three and twenty years had been insufficient to make his wife understand his character. Her mind was less difficult to develope. She was a woman of mean understanding, little information, and uncertain temper. When she was discontented, she fancied herself nervous. The business of her life was to find places in society, employment or rich wives for all her sons; its solace was visiting and news.

Chapter Two

Mr Bennet was among the earliest of those who waited on Mr Bingley. He had always intended to visit him, although to the last always assuring his wife that he should not go; and till the evening after the visit was paid, she had no knowledge of it. It was then disclosed in the following manner. Observing Edward employed in reading a book, Mr Bennet suddenly addressed him with,

"I hope Mr Bingley will approve of your taste in reading, Edward."

"We are not in a way to know what Mr Bingley likes," said Edward's mother resentfully, "since we are not to visit."

"But you forget, mama," said Edward, "That we shall meet him at the assemblies, and that Mrs Long has promised to introduce him."

"I do not believe Mrs Long will do any such thing. She has two nephews of her own, and no money for their advancement. She is a selfish, hypocritical woman, and I have no opinion of her."

"No more have I," said Mr Bennet, "and I am glad to find that you do not depend on her serving you."

Mrs Bennet deigned not to make any reply; but unable to contain herself, began scolding one of her sons.

"Don't keep coughing so, Charlie, for heaven's sake! Have a little compassion on my nerves. You tear them to pieces."

"Charlie has no discretion in his coughs said his father, "He times them ill."

"I do not cough for my own amusement," replied Charles fretfully.

"When is your next ball to be, Edward?"

"To-morrow fortnight."

"Aye, so it is," cried his mother, "and Mrs Long does not come back till the day before; so, it will be impossible for her to introduce him, for she will not know him herself."

"Then, my dear, you may have the advantage of your friend, and introduce Mr Bingley to her."

"Impossible, Mr Bennet, impossible, when I am not acquainted with him myself; how can you be so teasing?"

"I honour your circumspection. A fortnight's acquaintance is certainly very little. One cannot know what a man really is, or what he may be persuaded to do for one's family, by the end of a fortnight. But if we do not venture, somebody else will; and after all, Mrs Long and her nephews must stand their chance; and therefore, as she will think it an act of kindness, if you decline the offer, I will take it on myself."

Every one stared at Mr Bennet. Mrs Bennet said only, "Nonsense, nonsense!"

"What can be the meaning of that emphatic exclamation?" cried he. "Do you consider the forms of introduction, and the stress that is laid on them, as nonsense? I cannot quite agree with you there. What say you, Mark? For you studied hard with your tutors, and continue now that you are articled to your uncle Philips; studies which give rise to deep reflection, I doubt not, and you read great books, and make extracts."

Mark wished to say something very sensible, but knew not know.

"While Mark is adjusting his ideas," Mr Bennet continued, "let us return to Mr Bingley."

"I am sick of Mr Bingley," cried his wife.

"I am sorry to hear that; but why did you not tell me so before? If I had known as much this morning, I certainly would not have called on him. It is very unlucky; but as I have actually paid the visit, we cannot escape the acquaintance now."

The astonishment of his whole family was just what he wished; that of Mrs Bennet perhaps surpassing the rest; though when the first tumult of joy was over, she began to declare that it was what she had expected all the while.

"How good it was in you, my dear Mr Bennet! But I knew I should persuade you at last. I was sure you loved your boys too well to neglect the interest of such an acquaintance. Well, how pleased I am! And it is such a good joke too, that you should have gone this morning, and never said a word about it till now."

"Now, Charlie, you may cough as much as you chuse," said Mr Bennet, and, as he spoke, he left the room, fatigued with the raptures of his wife.

"What an excellent father you have, boys," said she when the door was shut. "I do not know how you will ever make him amends for his kindness; nor me either, for that matter. At our time of life, it is not so pleasant, I can tell you, to be making new acquaintance every day; but for your sakes, we would do any thing. Luke, my love, though you are the youngest, I dare say Mr Bingley's sisters will dance with you at the next ball."

"Oh!" said Luke stoutly, "I am not afraid; for though I am the youngest, I'm the tallest, and ladies like a taller man."

The rest of the evening was spent in conjecturing how soon Mr Bingley would return Mr Bennet's visit, and determining when they should invite all the Bingley family to dinner.

Chapter Three

Not all that Mrs Bennet, however, with the assistance of her five sons, could ask on the subject was sufficient to draw from her husband any satisfactory description of Mr Bingley, nor any indication of his inclination towards assisting unrelated young men into a suitable occupation. Nor was any information forthcoming about the quantity, marital status, or financial endowments of any Miss Bingleys. The family attacked their father in various ways; with barefaced questions, ingenious suppos-itions, and distant surmises, but he eluded the skill of them all; and they were at last obliged to accept the second-hand intel-ligence of their neighbour Lady Lucas. Her report was highly favourable. Sir William had been delighted with Mr Bingley. He was quite young, wonderfully handsome, extremely agreeable, and to crown the whole, he meant to be at the next assembly with a large party.

Nothing could be more delightful! To be fond of dancing was a certain step towards becoming part of Meryton society; and bringing a large party opened up possibilities for a number of Meryton's young people being well settled, so very lively hopes of Mr Bingley's generosity were entertained.

"I dare say Lady Lucas has foolish notions of Charlotte's being settled at Netherfield," said Mrs Bennet to her husband, "but I can get something from Mr Bingley for our boys, I shall have nothing to wish for."

In a few days, Mr Bingley returned Mr Bennet's visit, and sat about ten minutes with him in his library. With no idea that he was being regarded as the goose which would lay golden eggs to set the Bennet family up for life, Mr Bingley did not ask to meet the younger Bennets, and saw only their father. The rest of the family was somewhat more fortunate, for they had the ad-vantage of ascertaining from an upper window, that Mr Bingley wore a blue coat, and rode a black horse.

An invitation to dinner cunningly worded to encompass Mr Bingley's entire family was afterwards dispatched; and already had Mrs Bennet planned the courses that were to do credit to her housekeeping, when an answer arrived which deferred it all. Mr Bingley was obliged to be in town the following day, and consequently unable to accept the honour of their invitation, &c. Mrs Bennet was quite disconcerted. She could not imagine what business he could have in town so soon after his arrival in Hertfordshire; and she began to fear that he might be always flying about from one place to another, and never settled at Netherfield as he ought to be. Lady Lucas quieted her fears a little by starting the idea of his being gone to London to collect his sisters, and to get up a large party for the ball; and a report soon followed that Mr Bingley was to bring twelve ladies and seven gentlemen with him to the assembly. The Bennets grieved over such a number of excess gentlemen, but were pleased to think there would be so many ladies available to dance with; but all this grieving was beforehand, as they found out the day before the ball, that instead of twelve ladies and seven gentlemen, he had brought only six in total with him from London, his five sisters and his cousin. This was still good news for the Bennet sons, and Mrs Bennet hoped that this cousin was also a man of fortune and influence. But when the Netherfield party entered the assembly room, it consisted of only five all together; Mr Bingley, his two sisters, the husband of the eldest, and the best friend of the youngest.

Mr Bingley was good looking and gentleman-like; he had a pleasant countenance and easy, unaffected manners. His sisters were fine women with an air of decided fashion. His brother-in-law, Mr Hurst, merely looked the gentleman, and moreover did not dance, joining the card players instead. Miss Bingley's best friend, Miss Darcy, soon drew the attention of all the young men in the room by her graceful figure, the rich lace on her gown, and the report which was in general circulation within five minutes after her entrance, of her being a great heiress from the north of England. She was pronounced to be the most beautiful creature ever seen, much handsomer than Miss Bingley or Mrs Hurst, and she was looked at with great admiration for about half the evening. Unfortunately, on her refusing to dance with anyone except Mr Bingley, she was discovered to be proud, to be above her company, and above being pleased with all the handsome young men of Meryton. And not all her great fortune could save her from having a most forbidding, disagreeable countenance as she refused the offers to stand up with one young man after another. Miss Bingley or Mrs Hurst stepped in every time, and accepted in Miss Darcy's stead, and were much praised for their alacrity and willingness to dance.

Mr Bingley had soon made himself acquainted with all the principal people in the room and introduced his party; he was lively and unreserved, danced every dance, was angry that the ball closed so early, and talked of giving one himself at Netherfield. Such amiable qualities must speak for themselves, and showed Miss Darcy up in an increasingly poor light by comparison; she was held to be an unworthy addition to the Bingley party, and not likely to add much to the enjoyment of the neighbourhood.

When John led Miss Bingley into the next set, Edward, feeling sorry for Miss Darcy sitting alone, went to ask for her hand into the dance, but she refused with some confusion and begged him instead to sit down beside her.

"I regret Mr Bennet," she said, with her face turned down, "that my brother does not wish for me to dance with any body but Mr Bingley or Mr Hurst, and Mr Bingley is much engaged with the other young ladies, and Mr Hurst – "

"Mr Hurst does not dance, I see," Edward said. "It is of no matter; I am happy to sit out this set and rest my feet."

They were both silent for a moment before Edward's curiosity prompted him to say, "Your brother is very anxious for your health, that he does not wish you to dance with any one but his friends?"

"Indeed," Miss Darcy replied, "he is a very good brother and very concerned about me, but I do wish –"

She did not complete the thought, and Edward took pity on her and turned the subject.

Indeed, they found conversation with each other most engrossing and satisfying and did not notice the end of the dance and Miss Bingley's return. She saw them sitting together and when Edward stood to bow as she approached, she took his seat, and angled her back to him so that he could no longer speak with Miss Darcy, nor engage Miss Bingley's attention.

Edward started to move off, but caught Miss Bingley saying to Miss Darcy, "I apologise for leaving you alone; I did not think you would be bothered by that young man."

Edward could not hear Miss Darcy's reply.

"No indeed, think of your brother," Miss Bingley continued, "he does not wish for you to be a target for younger sons and fortune hunters."

Edward walked away with no very cordial feelings towards Miss Bingley. He told an expurgated version of the story to Charlotte Lucas, who was always ready to dance with and listen to the Bennets, with great spirit, for he had a lively, playful disposition, which delighted in anything ridiculous. And he found that he cared not for Miss Bingley's ill opinion of him, as Miss Darcy had been most agreeable to him before her interruption, and he had felt that they had conversed very comfortably and easily.

"Then, Miss Bingley does not know of your true circumstances?" Charlotte enquired.

"No, indeed, nor Miss Darcy. I have a strange fancy that I prefer to be judged by my own merits," Edward replied, "I beg you will not enlighten either one of them." Charlotte agreed to keep his secret should she become intimate with either Miss Bingley or Miss Darcy, "But," she added, "it cannot be long before some body tells them."

"I will face that when it happens, but not before," Edward said, and they carried on down the dance in perfect amity, unaware of Mrs Bennet's scowl; she had long suspected the Lucases of conniving at marrying Charlotte to one of her precious boys, and this suspicion had not altered with the arrival of the single and wealthy Mr Bingley; for Charlotte had no looks, or fortune to recommend her, and she doubted Mr

Bingley would notice her amongst all the other beauties of the neighbourhood.

Despite these little rubs, the evening passed off pleasantly for the whole family. Mrs Bennet had been her eldest son much in Mr Bingley's company, and dancing with both his sisters. John himself was as much gratified by Mr Bingley's notice and Miss Bingley's complaisance as his mother could be, though in a quieter way, and Edward felt John's pleasure. Their peculiar circumstances meant that they had been much divided during their early youth, and the last few weeks had been doubly precious, bringing them back together before they would have to part for good.

Mark had heard himself mentioned as a true scholar, and the most well-read young man in the neighbourhood; and Charles and Luke had been fortunate enough to be never without partners, which was all that they had yet learnt to care for at a ball.

They returned therefore in good spirits to Longbourn, the village where they lived, and of which they were the principal inhabitants. They found Mr Bennet still up. With a book he was regardless of time; and on the present occasion he had a good deal of curiosity as to the event of an evening which had raised such splendid expectations. He had rather hoped that all his wife's views on the stranger would be disappointed; but he soon found that he had a very different story to hear.

"Oh! My dear Mr Bennet," as she entered the room, "we have had a most delightful evening, a most excellent ball. John was so admired; nothing could be like it. I wish you had been there to see how he looked as though he were a member of their family already. Mr Bingley danced first with Miss Lucas; I was so vexed to see him stand up with her. You know how encroaching those Lucases can be; they want nothing but the best for Charlotte. However, he did not admire her at all: indeed no body can, you know; and he danced with all the other young ladies without distinguishing any of them. Miss Bingley, and Mrs Hurst danced with every body who asked; they were most obliging indeed, and Mrs Hurst is a most charming woman. I never in my life saw any thing more elegant than their dresses. I dare say the lace upon Miss Darcy's gown –"

Here she was interrupted. Mr Bennet protested against any description of finery. She was therefore obliged to seek another branch of the subject, and related, with much bitterness of spirit and some exaggeration, the shocking rudeness of Miss Darcy in refusing to stand up with Edward, and Miss Bingley's comment about him being a fortune hunter.

"But I can assure you that Eddie does not lose much by not suiting Miss Darcy's fancy; for she is too high for her company, and most disagreeable despite her fortune. I wish you had been there, my dear, to give her one of your set-downs. I quite detest that woman."

Chapter Four

When Edward and John were alone, they discussed their feelings about the Bingley party. Mr Bingley came in for general praise.

"He is such a man as I should model myself upon, and look to as a mentor," John said, "he is sensible, good-humoured, lively; so much ease, with such perfect good breeding. I do hope he will settle at Netherfield, and that we might become friends."

Mrs and Mr Hurst were dismissed as not likely to add materially to either one's happiness, education or future, but both allowed that they were well-bred and friendly enough.

Miss Bingley was, however, the subject of some dispute. John had found her amiable, even gracious, and she had danced twice with him; on both occasions conversing lightly and knowledgeably about current events and modern literature. He had been most impressed with her, and hoped she carried away a favourable impression home of him.

"Well," Edward said, "she may have approved of you, but she did not approve of me. Still, I give you leave to like her if you will. For if Mr Bingley does not marry, her children stand to inherit his fortune and house," and before John could tell him off for being mercenary, Edward added, "and you have liked many a stupider person!"

"Dear Edward!"

"Oh! You are a good deal too apt you know, to like people in general. You never see a fault in any body. All the world are good and agreeable in your eyes. I never heard you speak ill of a human being in my life."

"I would wish not to be hasty in censuring any one," John began.

"Unlike Miss Bingley," Edward cut in. "She knows nothing of my circumstances, nor my intentions towards her friend, which were, by the by, entirely honourable. I needed a rest from dancing, and she was obliged to sit out, so we kept each other company. That was all, but Miss Bingley assumed wrongly –"

"Indeed, it was good of you to sit with Miss Darcy, and a shame that she was not permitted to stand up with any body except her own party."

"I wonder at her brother's lack of trust," Edward mused, "can it be that he does not trust the Bingleys and Hursts not to take her into company that he would not approve himself? It does not seem likely that they would take her any where that might cause her distress."

"He is clearly very protective of her."

"Maybe it is as Miss Bingley hinted, that she has been prey to fortune hunters. It is said she has thirty thousand pounds, which would be quite an incentive for an unscrupulous man."

"Poor Miss and Mr Darcy," John said, his face clouding at the thought of anyone insinuating themselves into Miss Darcy's company with such low motives.

He turned the conversation back to Miss Bingley and the favourable impression she had given him.

Edward listened in silence. He had not thought that either Miss Bingley, nor Mrs Hurst's manners were equal to their brother's. Although seemingly complaisant, and willing to dance, their behaviour at the assembly had not been calculated to please in general; and with more quickness of observation and less pliancy of temper than John, and with a judgement too unassailed by any attention to himself, Edward was very little disposed to approve them. They were indeed very fine ladies; not deficient in good humour, as was clear from their dancing with any body who requested their hand, but they seemed to him proud and conceited. They were both rather handsome, had been educated in one of the first private seminaries in town, had a fortune each of twenty thousand pounds, were in the habit of spending more than they ought, and of associating with people of rank; and were therefore in every respect entitled to think well of themselves, and meanly of others. They were of a respectable family in the north of England; a circumstance more deeply impressed on their memories than that their brother's fortune, and their own, had been acquired by trade.

Mr Bingley inherited property to the amount of nearly an hundred thousand pounds from his father, who had intended to purchase an estate, but did not live to do it. Mr Bingley intended it likewise, and sometimes made choice of his county; but as he was now provided with a good house and the liberty of a manor, it was doubtful to many of those who best knew the easiness of his temper, whether he might not spend the remainder of his days at Netherfield, and leave the next generation to purchase, were he inclined to marry at all.

His sisters were very anxious for his having an estate of his own; but though he was now established only as a tenant, Miss Bingley was by no means unwilling to preside at his table, nor was Mrs Hurst, who had married a man of more fashion than fortune, less disposed to consider his house as her home when it suited her. Mr Bingley had not been of age two years, when he was tempted by an accidental recommendation to look at Netherfield House. He did look at it and into it for half an hour, was pleased with the situation and the principal rooms, was satisfied with what the owner said in its praise, and took it immediately.

Miss Darcy was frequently staying with Miss Bingley, who considered her a most intimate friend. Miss Darcy was too shy, and thought too little of herself to resist Miss Bingley's stronger character. Her brother and Miss Bingley, both had hopes that Mr Bingley and Miss Darcy would settle down together on an estate bordering Pemberley, where Darcy had his seat. If Miss Darcy or Mr Bingley was aware of their siblings' plans, they gave no sign of it, and treated each other as brother and sister. Miss Bingley's motives were not entirely altruistic though; she also hoped that a close alliance between the two families might result in Darcy's making her an offer as well.

As for Bingley and Darcy's friendship; it was a very long-lasting and steady friendship, in spite of a great opposition of character. Bingley was endeared to Darcy by the easiness, openness, ductility of his temper, though no disposition could offer a greater contrast to his own, and though with his own he never appeared dissatisfied. On the strength of Darcy's regard Bingley had the firmest reliance, and of his judgement the highest opinion. It was a credit to Mr Bingley's trustworthiness that Mr Darcy allowed his sister to spend time in Bingley's house; and to know that she would be perfectly safe with his family.

Mrs Hurst and Miss Bingley were less enamoured of Meryton society than their brother; but Netherfield was set in sufficiently large grounds for them to be able to avoid most of the people they had met at the assembly, most of the time, and was grand enough to satisfy their ambitions for the time being.

Chapter Five

Within a short walk of Longbourn lived a family with whom the Bennets were particularly intimate. Sir William Lucas had been formerly in trade in Meryton, where he had made a tolerable fortune and risen to the honour of knighthood by an address to the King, during his mayoralty. The distinction had perhaps been felt too strongly. It had given him a disgust to his business and to his residence in a small market town; and quitting them both, he had removed with his family to a house about a mile from Meryton, denominated from that period Lucas Lodge, where he could think with pleasure of his own importance, and unshackled by business, occupy himself solely in being civil to all the world. For though elated by his rank, it did not render him supercilious; on the contrary, he was all attention to every body. By nature inoffensive, friendly and obliging, his presentation at St James's had made him courteous.

Lady Lucas was a very good kind of woman, not too clever to be a valuable neighbour to Mrs Bennet. They had several children. The eldest of them, a sensible, intelligent young woman, about twenty-seven, was the Charlotte that Mrs Bennet suspected of casting her eyes at her own older sons, and of being cast by her parents at Mr Bingley. The eldest Bennets and Lucases had been childhood playmates, and considered themselves quite brothers and sisters.

That the Lucases should visit the Bennets to talk over a ball was absolutely necessary; and the morning after the assembly brought the former to Longbourn to hear and to communicate.

"You began the evening well, Charlotte," said Mrs Bennet with civil self-command to Miss Lucas, "You were Mr Bingley's first choice."

"But he did not ask me again, and danced with every young woman in the room, it seemed."

"Ah yes, I did observe that, to be sure. But he was much taken with John, and talked with him for a long time. I believe it was so, I heard something about it – but I hardly know what – something about Mr Robinson."

"Perhaps you mean what I overheard between Mr Bingley and

Mr Robinson; did not I mention it to you? Mr Robinson's asking Mr Bingley how he liked our Meryton assemblies, and whether he did not think there were a great many pretty women in the room, and whether he thought to have made some friends amongst the young men? And his answering immediately to the last question – Oh! The eldest Mr Bennet beyond a doubt was a man after his own heart and one that would become a close friend to all his family for sure."

"Upon my word! Well, that was very decided indeed – that does seem as if – but however, it may all come to nothing you know."

"My overhearings were more to the purpose than yours, Eddie," said Charlotte, "Miss Bingley was not so well worth listening to as her brother, was she? Poor Eddie! To be despised as a poor younger son desperate to get his hands on an heiress's wealth!"

"I beg you will not put it into Edward's head to be vexed with Miss Bingley; she was most gracious to John, and Mr Bingley will listen to her good opinion of John, I am sure. As for Miss Darcy; whatever was she about? Mrs Long told me last night that she sat by Miss Darcy for half an hour without her once opening her lips."

"Are you quite sure, Ma'am? Is not there a little mistake?" said John, "I certainly saw Miss Darcy speaking to Mrs Long."

"Aye, because she begged leave to introduce her nephews to Miss Darcy as dance partners, and Miss Darcy could not help answering her, but Mrs Long said she seemed very angry at being appealed to."

Edward was not sure if he was authorised to tell the company that Miss Darcy had been forbidden by her brother to stand up with any body but the members of her own party; and decided upon reflection that Miss Darcy had not given him leave to make such information general knowledge.

"Miss Bingley informed me that Miss Darcy is most agreeable amongst her intimate acquaintance," John said.

"I do not believe a word of it, my dear. Is she was so very agreeable, she would have talked to Mrs Long, and stood up with Edward, and with Mrs Long's nephews, and any body else who asked. But I dare say she is ate up with pride because of her brother's and her own fortunes, and had heard somehow that Mrs Long does not keep a carriage, and had come to the ball in a hack chaise."

Edward, who had not found Miss Darcy in any way proud, found it hard not to come to her defence, and attempted to turn the subject; but the women were not finished on the subject of Miss Darcy.

"Her pride," said Miss Lucas, "does not offend me as much as pride often does, because there is an excuse for it. One cannot wonder that so very rich a young woman, with family, fortune, every thing in her favour, should keep herself exclusive. If I may so express it, she has a right to be proud."

"That is very true," Edward replied, "but I could thank Miss Bingley for not supposing I was a fortune hunter, and mortifying my pride!"

"Pride," observed Mark, who piqued himself on the breadth of his reading, and the solidity of his reflections, "is a very common failing, I believe. By all that I have ever read, I am convinced that it is very common indeed, that human nature is particularly prone to it, and that there are very few of us who do not cherish a feeling of self-complacency on the score of some quality or other, real or imaginary. Vanity and pride are different things, though the words are often used synonymously. A person may be proud without being vain. Pride relates more to our opinion of ourselves, vanity to what we would have others think of us."

At this point a younger Lucas gave way to his feelings of boredom at being confined indoors on such a sunny day and began to kick at the furniture, and the Lucas family took their leave.

Chapter Six

John and Mr Bingley were soon in frequent communication, visiting to and fro from Longbourn and Netherfield. Bingley held shooting parties, and as John was leaving one day to join the party, Mrs Bennet called out,

"John! Tell Mr Bingley that when he has killed all his own birds, he may come here and shoot as many as he please, on Mr Bennet's manor. I am sure we will be vastly happy to oblige him, and I will prevail on Mr Bennet to save all the best covies for him."

On occasion, Mr Bingley prevailed upon his sisters to accompany him to Longbourn, and they were willing enough to meet John and even Edward, but the mother was found to be intolerable, and the younger brothers not worth speaking to. Miss Darcy was never included in the party to visit Longbourn, however, Miss Bingley could not keep her from being in the company when John and Edward visited their brother.

On these occasions, Miss Darcy received Edward's attentions with every evidence of pleasure, and they spent many hours discussing books and paintings, exhibitions, travel, education of the estate workers at Pemberley, and poetry, with Miss Darcy beginning to blossom under the regard of someone who was genuinely interested in her opinion, and took her recommendations away to look up for himself. These short, stolen meetings did not pass unobserved by Miss Bingley, who persuaded her brother to write to Mr Darcy to hasten his visit to Netherfield, to save his sister from a grasping young man from a local family that was notorious for being both necessitous and numerous.

For John, the attention from Miss Bingley and her brother was received with the greatest pleasure; but Edward still saw superciliousness in her treatment of every body, hardly excepting even John, and could not like her.

By some miracle, no body had told Miss Bingley or Miss Darcy about Edward's true situation, and he was determined to become a friend to Miss Darcy without the stain of fortune tainting their discourse, but it became harder and harder to get access to her, even though, when they did meet, he began to suspect that she was viewing him as more than just a friend.

As he had been accustomed to do as a child, Edward took his concerns to Charlotte Lucas, regarding her quite as an older sister and one who would understand another woman far better than he could ever do.

"I cannot tell if Miss Darcy looks upon me just as a   welcome relief from the small circle she is confined to at Netherfield, or if the composure of her temper and uniform cheerfulness of her manner towards me, guards her from the impertinent suspicions of Miss Bingley, but hides a strength of feeling."

"it may perhaps be necessary," said Charlotte, "to hide one's feelings in such a case as Miss Darcy's; but it is sometimes a disadvantage to be so guarded. If a woman conceals her affection with the same skill from the object of it, she may lose the opportunity of fixing him; and it will then be but poor consolation to believe the rest of the world equally in the dark."

Edward was not sure whether to be amused or shocked. "Is this part of a gently reared female's education?" he enquired, "How to fix a man?"

Charlotte was not to be deterred by raillery, "There is so much of gratitude or vanity in almost every attachment, that it is not safe to leave any to itself. We can all begin freely – a slight preference is natural enough; but there are very few of us who have heart enough to be really in love without encouragement."

"It is hard to encourage Miss Darcy, when she is being kept from seeing me," Edward said. "Miss Bingley still thinks I am an impecunious second son who is on the hunt for a credulous heiress. Although we meet tolerably often, it is not for very long before Miss Bingley intervenes and takes Miss Darcy off for some trumped up reason or other. Or we are in large mixed parties and it is impossible that every moment should be employed in conversing together; our commitments to others in the party must also be attended to."

"And have you learned much of Miss Darcy's preferences in your interrupted time together?"

"I have been able to ascertain that we share much of the same taste in literature, painting, and outdoor pursuits, and we converse very freely and easily."

"Well," said Charlotte, "if you were to be married to Miss Darcy tomorrow, you would have as good a chance of happiness as if you were to be studying each other's character for a twelve-month. Happiness in marriage is entirely a matter of chance. If the dispositions of the parties are ever so well known to each other, or ever so similar before-hand, it does not advance their felicity in the least. They always continue to grow sufficiently unlike afterwards to have their share of vexation; and it is better to know as little as possible of the defects of the person with whom you are to pass your life."

"You make me laugh, Charlotte; but it is not sound. You know it is not sound, and that you would never act this way yourself."

Occupied in attempting to thwart Miss Bingley, and gain access to Miss Darcy, all the while keeping from both that he was about to inherit a large fortune and a country house in Derbyshire, Edward was unaware of his former playmate's own heart-ache. Charlotte was approaching the age of danger, and no closer to fixing a man than she had been since she came out, despite her philosophy on marriage. Meryton society was small, and there were few eligible men who could afford a wife with no fortune. She knew both John and Edward regarded her as their sister, and suspected that would never change. But she watched John's tentative approaches to Miss Bingley with a real concern, that he could not see what was clear to Charlotte; that John was not rich enough for Miss Bingley to do more than pass an idle moment with, or dance with at a local assembly.

To every body's surprise, Miss Darcy attended the next large party at Lucas Lodge, having secured an invitation by a visit to Lady Lucas shortly after Mr Darcy's arrival. Edward was introduced to Mr Darcy by his sister, who declined to do more than acknowledge Edward with a slight bow, soon after walking away and taking Miss Darcy with him.

Edward moved on to talk to Sir William, and to thank him for convening this party, while Charlotte invited the ladies present to perform at the piano. Maria Lucas, at the request of Charles and Luke Bennet, played some lively Scotch and Irish airs, at which the furniture was pushed back, and several couples joined eagerly in dancing at one end of the room.

Mr Darcy was standing with his sister in silent indignation at such a mode of passing the evening, and was more than thankful to Miss Bingley for persuading her brother to alert him to the dangers to his sister in such society. He was contemplating an early withdrawal from the party, when Sir William arrived at his side and said,

"What a charming amusement for young people this is, Mr Darcy! There is nothing like dancing after all. I consider it as one of the first refinements of polished societies."

"Certainly sir, and it has the advantage also of being in vogue amongst the less polished societies of the world – Every savage can dance."

Sir William only smiled. "I am sure Miss Darcy would like to join the other young people," he said, noticing Mr Bingley join the dancers, "And I doubt not that you are an adept at the science yourself, Mr Darcy. Do you often dance at St James's?"

"Never, Sir."

"Do you not think it would be a proper compliment to the place?"

"It is a compliment which I never pay to any place if I can avoid it."

"You have a house in town, I conclude?"

Mr Darcy bowed.

"I had once some thoughts of fixing in town myself – for I am fond of superior society; but I did not feel quite certain that the air of London would agree with Lady Lucas."

He paused in hopes of an answer; but Mr Darcy was not disposed to make any, and Sir William realised that Edward Bennet was still standing on his other side. He was struck with the notion of doing a very gallant thing, and turned to Miss Darcy.

"My dear Miss Darcy, why are you not dancing? You will allow me to present this young man as a very desirable partner, unless you would wish one of my own sons to partner you?" He held out one hand to Miss Darcy and the other to Edward, who though surprised was very willing to receive it, but Mr Darcy intervened, taking his sister's hand and tucking it under his own arm.

"Indeed, Sir, my sister does not intend to dance," Mr Darcy said, bowed to Sir William, and moved away, leaving Edward and Sir William rather surprised and not a little disconcerted.

Mr Darcy took his sister over to Miss Bingley and murmured a request to escort both ladies back to Netherfield.

She was quite in agreement, "Indeed, Mr Darcy, it is insupportable to pass many evenings in this manner – in such society; indeed I am quite of your opinion. I was never more annoyed! The insipidity and yet the noise; the nothingness and yet the self-importance of all these people! What I would give to hear your strictures on them!"

But Mr Darcy would not be drawn beyond supposing that his sister was tired, and that they had stayed long enough to fulfil the requirements of propriety, as he led his sister and his party out to their carriage.

Chapter Seven

Mr Bennet's property consisted almost entirely in an estate of two thousand a year, which had been entailed on a male heir, and Mrs Bennet's fortune, although ample for her situation in life, could but ill supply the deficiency in his. Her father had been an attorney in Meryton, and had left her four thousand pounds.

She had a sister married to a Mr Philips, who had been a clerk to their father, and succeeded him in the business, and a brother settled in London in a respectable line of trade.

It had therefore been a source of considerable relief to both Mr and Mrs Bennet when a son was born within a year of their marriage. Named John, this son was a blessing, and saved the estate from being passed on to a distant cousin. The arrival of a second son a year or so later provided the security of knowing that should anything untoward happen to his older brother, he could step into the breach and end the entail just as efficiently. It is generally considered wise for a woman to provide her husband with an heir and a spare if at all possible. Should John survive into his majority, Edward had been named after Mrs Bennet's brother, in the hope that he might be apprenticed to that successful business one day.

However, once the third son arrived, there was far less rejoicing and much more discussion about whether a third son could ever inherit, with two lives between him and the estate in question. It was unlikely, but not completely impossible, given the infant mortality rate, and occasional sheer bad luck. But it remained unlikely, and Mark would probably have to shift for himself when he grew up, particularly as the Bennets had no influence in the Church, the Army, or the Navy, and no spare money to buy a commission for him, even if he were martially minded. Mark was a less robust baby than his brothers, but he clung to life, and eventually prospered. It seemed that the Bennets were not only blessed with sons, but with healthy sons who thrived and looked set to reach adulthood.

Mr Bennet may have hoped for a daughter, but instead, when his lady presented him with two more sons, Charles and Luke, it was seen as more of a tragedy than a triumph, and the fate of these supernumerary sons was much discussed in the drawing rooms of all their friends and acquaintances. Mr Bennet's estate was a good enough one to pass on to one son, but it was not a big enough estate to support four younger brothers, especially if John wished to marry in order to secure the succession with a son of his own. The other four sons would have to either shift for themselves and find their own occupation, or hope to secure a rich wife.

The Bennet boys' looks and characters were apparent from a young age.

John, the eldest, was a handsome boy, placid and good-natured.

He was a source of great pride to Mrs Bennet, who was sure that someone so handsome must make a very good marriage and so raise the fortunes of the whole family. She kept a wary eye on Lady Lucas, who had daughters close to John's age, and Mrs Bennet was sure the Lucases had designated John as the husband who would raise their own family's fortunes, which were certainly not as good as the Bennets'.

Edward, next in birth and beauty, was a livelier boy than John. He was the apple of his father's eye, who saw in Edward a kindred spirit, someone intelligent enough to understand his father, and to appreciate a position in the centre of his father's life. It was a shame, to be sure, that Edward was not the eldest, but maybe that position with Mr Gardiner could be sought for him when he finished his schooling.

Mr Bennet applied himself with unusual energy to the schooling of his first two sons. Both must be educated as gentlemen, and both must end their schooling with a full understanding of estate management, accounting, and subjects suitable for a gentleman to secure their place in good society. Mr Bennet intended both to go on to University where they would make useful acquaintances, and possibly meet with patronage, or the rich sisters of their University fellows.

In the end, only John went on to University.

Fate intervened for Edward in the shape of distant relatives of Mr Bennet; Mr and Mrs Fellowes, who were very rich, but childless. They offered to adopt Edward as their only son, and to pass on their wealth to him in due course. Mr and Mrs Bennet could not do other than accept; Mrs Bennet's brother had inconsiderately married and had sons of his own to bring into his own business, and Edward was not minded to go into the retail trade any way. Thus, John went to Oxford, and Edward went to London; but Mr and Mrs Fellowes were indulgent parents and Edward was able to visit the Bennets whenever he wished, and to stay for many weeks at a time. Mr Fellowes was in the process of winding up his business interests in London, intending to retire, and buy a country estate, which would become his son's in due course. John was down from University, and so Edward was at his childhood home, probably for the last time.

Mark, next in line, seemed to be a magnet for all the childhood ailments, but recovered from each one little the worst for the experience. One bout of measles left his eye-sight poor, and a Doctor was consulted who suggested spectacles, which did not assist with Mark's already plain looks by comparison with his brothers. Indeed, Mark would have been a well-looking boy in any other family, but his mild looks waned into insignificance beside his brothers, especially John, and caused Mrs Bennet considerable disappointment, which she seldom failed to express whenever Mark caught her eye.

Mr Bennet's activity and indeed his necessity for arranging education for his sons was quite worn out by the time Mark was old enough to need more schooling than a very young tutor could provide; but Mark himself quietly persisted in requesting more formal education than could be gleaned by dipping into his father's books. He went first in the family to a nearby Grammar school, and spent all his spare time in study at home as well. He was a favourite of his Uncle and Aunt Philips who had no children of their own, and his future was set to be articled to Mr Philips's firm. Although studious and well-behaved, Mark had not the gentleness of John, nor the well-modulated liveliness of Edward, and Mr Bennet found his seriousness rather turgid, especially after he came under the influence of a teacher who introduced him to Fordyce's Sermons, and to epigrams. There was no meeting of minds for Mr Bennet and his middle son, although Mr Bennet did allow Mark to borrow books from his own study once he realised the books would be safe with him.

Charles and Luke were so similar that they often seemed like twins, and were usually treated as a pair, rather than individuals. Charles was very much under Luke's influence, and was a rather sickly child, given to minor ailments, which lingered. He had some of his eldest brothers' good-looks, but toned down, so that he was a pale copy of them. His constant snuffling and coughing caused much irritation to both his parents, and his peevish response to their criticisms did not further endear him. Neither he nor Luke had any interest in education, and their father retreated into his study, leaving them to their mother's care. They were as yet full young for their future occupation to be fixed; but some thing would have to be sought for them sooner rather than later.

The loss of Edward had affected Mr Bennet more than any body realised, and he lived for the times when his eldest two sons would be home again.

Although laconic in his expressions of pleasure, he felt their importance in the family circle. Evening conversation, in particular, lost much of its animation, and almost all its sense, when John and Edward were absent; although there would come a time very soon when Edward would return no more, being settled with Mr and Mrs Fellowes on their country estate.

To every body's surprize, Mrs Bennet had been persuaded not to speak of Edward's good fortune until the matter was entirely settled by the Fellowes' London attorney. She felt in two minds about it, and remained uncertain whether to crow over her son being chosen in this way, or feel ashamed for the disgrace attendant on the Bennets' estate not being large enough to support more than one son; there was also the fear that she might be judged harshly for giving away one of her children. Edward had told Charlotte Lucas, but she too was enjoined to secrecy until such a time as the news became general.

Luke was his mother's favourite. Born last, but firmly determined not to let that stand in the way of his own amusement, Luke was handsome, loud, boisterous and uninhibited. Edward in particular attempted to tone down some of his wildness, and instruct him in the proper behaviour when in society. However, Edward's efforts were met with wide-eyed incomprehension, and his mother made no attempt to modify Luke's behaviour: she rather encouraged it, made him lots of presents and laughed at all his jokes.

As for Mrs Bennet, once it became clear there would be no more children; she threw herself into the social life of Meryton, with her two youngest sons as her escorts, for Mr Bennet did not care to go out as often as his wife would like. Charles and Luke were very popular in and around Meryton for their high spirits and willingness to participate in any high jinks or jokes that were perpetrated by the younger people. Mrs Bennet kept a sharp eye out for designing mamas looking to marry off their daughters into Longbourn's principal family, but younger sons were never so attractive to a match-making mama, so Charles and Luke were free to enjoy female company without giving rise to any expectations.

The village of Longbourn was only a mile from Meryton; a most convenient distance for the younger Bennets, who were usually tempted thither three or four times a week, nominally to pay their respects to their Uncle and Aunt, but actually to take part in any mischief or merry making that they could encounter. Charles and Luke were particularly frequent in these attentions; their minds were more vacant than their brothers', and when nothing better offered, a walk to Meryton was necessary to amuse their morning hours and furnish conversation for the evening; and however bare of news the country in general might be, they always contrived to learn some from their aunt. At present, indeed, they were well supplied both with news and happiness by the recent arrival of a militia regiment in the neighbourhood; it was to remain the whole winter, and Meryton was the Head Quarters.

Their visits to Mrs Philips were now productive of the most interesting intelligence. Every day added something to their knowledge of the officers' names and connections. Their lodgings were not long a secret, and at length they began to know the officers themselves. Mr Philips visited them all, and this opened to his nephews a source of felicity unknown before. They could talk of nothing but militia and officers, and Mr Bingley's large fortune, the mention of which gave   animation to their mother's eyes, was worthless in their eyes when opposed to the regimentals of an ensign. Mr Bingley might have been able to make his way back into their esteem if he were to confess to any influence at all in the militia, but he had yet to do so, and thus was overlooked as a source of felicity by Charles and Luke.

After listening to their effusions on the subject of warfare and regimentals, Mr Bennet coolly observed,

"From all that I can collect by your manner of talking, you must be two of the silliest young men in the county. I have suspected it some time, but now I am convinced."

Charles was disconcerted by this direct opposition, and made no answer, but Luke, with perfect indifference, continued to express his admiration of all Britain's fighting men, and especially their very smart uniforms.

"I am astonished, my dear," said Mrs Bennet, "that you should be so ready to think your own children silly. If I wished to think slightingly of any body's children, it would not be of my own however."

"If my children are silly, I must hope to be always sensible of it."

"Yes – but as it happens, they are all of them very clever."

"This is the only point, I flatter myself, on which we do not agree. I had hoped that our sentiments coincided in every particular, but I must so far differ from you to think our two youngest sons uncommonly foolish."

"My dear Mr Bennet, you must not expect young boys to have the sense of their father and mother. When they get to our age, I dare say they will not think warfare and soldiery so exciting any more than we do. I thought all the officers looked most becoming in their regimentals the other night at Sir William's."

"Mama," cried Luke, "my aunt says that Colonel Forster and Captain Carter do not go so often to Miss Watson's as they did when they first came; she sees them now very often standing in Clarke's library."

Mrs Bennet was prevented from replying by the entrance of the footman with a note for John; it was from Netherfield, and the servant waited for an answer.

Chapter Eight

Mrs Bennet's eyes sparkled with pleasure, and she was eagerly calling out, even as John was reading the note.

"Well, John, who is it from? What it is about? What does Mr Bingley say? Well, John, make haste and tell us; make haste my love."

"It is from Mr Bingley, as you surmise, Mama, to Edward as well," said John, and then read it aloud.

"My dear friends

Darcy, Hurst and I are to dine with the officers this evening, and we extend an invitation to join our party.

Yours

Charles Bingley"

John handed the note to Edward, who said, 'There is more, but Mr Bingley's hand-writing is most difficult to make out. He leaves out many words and blots the rest!"

"Dining with the officers!" cried Luke. "I wonder my aunt did not tell us of that."

"Dining out with the officers," said Mrs Bennet, "That is very unlucky indeed."

"How so, my dear?" inquired Mr Bennet, "How can an invitation to dine out be unlucky for our sons?"

"Well, Miss Bingley will not be of the party," said his mother, with lots of significant nods at John.

"However, you can take this chance to ask her brother if she has an understanding with any body."

"Mama! I could not do that!"

"Oh! very well. But mind you ask him if he intends to stay at Netherfield. He has only a short lease."

"Very well," said John, "If the opportunity should arise, I will ask him."

"Good. Well, well, dining with the officers. It looks as though Mr Bingley or Mr Darcy might have some influence there after all."

"May we come too?" Luke asked, but Edward shook his head.

"No indeed, the invitation from Mr Bingley is for us only. If you wish to be invited, you must seek an   invitation from your own friends."

Luke pouted, but then cast a very meaningful look at Charles, and both left the room, heads together.

Edward heard Luke say to Charles, "If we make haste, perhaps we may see something of Colonel Forster before he attends the dinner."

"May we have the carriage?" said John.

"Indeed, I think you must," Mrs Bennet said, "For the gentlemen will have Mr Bingley's chaise to go to   Meryton, and the Hursts have no horses to theirs. I am sure your father can spare the horses."

"Are the horses wanted on the farm?" Edward enquired of his father.

"They are wanted on the farm much oftener than I can get them," was the response, "but you must arrive like gentlemen if you are to dine with the officers."

The two had not been long gone when it rained hard, and continued the whole evening without   intermission.

"There," Mrs Bennet said with satisfaction, "I knew they needed the carriage. You are very good to spare the horses, Mr Bennet."

. **

The dinner with the officers was more formal and less debauched than Edward had feared. There were no women present, but the officers of the – shire were in general a very creditable, gentlemanlike set, and the best of them were of the present party; the conversation was wide-ranging, and convivial.

Edward and John were seated near Mr Bingley and across from Mr Darcy and Mr Hurst.

John kept his promise to his mother to ask Mr Bingley if he intended to keep on at Netherfield once his short lease was over.

"Whatever I do is done in a hurry," replied he; "and therefore if I should resolve to quit Netherfield, I should probably be off in five minutes. At present, however, I consider myself as quite fixed here."

"That is exactly what I should have supposed of you," said Edward.

"You begin to comprehend me, do you?" cried he,   turning towards Edward and raising his glass in salute.

"Oh! Yes – I understand you perfectly."

"I wish I might take this for a compliment; but to be so easily seen through I am afraid is pitiable."

"That is as it happens. It does not necessarily follow that a deep, intricate character is more or less estimable than such a one as yours."

"I did not know before," continued Bingley, "that you were a studier of character. It must be an amusing study."

"Yes; but intricate characters are the most amusing. They have at least that advantage."

Mr Darcy leaned forward to join in the conversation over the table.

"The country," said he, "can in general supply but few subjects for such a study. In a country neighbourhood you move in very confined and unvarying society."

"But people themselves alter so much, that there is something new to be observed in them forever."

Darcy bowed his head coldly, and turned back to speak with his neighbour.

"When I am in the country," said Bingley, "I never wish to leave it; and when I am in town it is pretty much the same. They have each their advantages, and I can be equally happy in either."

"That's because you have the right disposition," said John.

"It is very easy to be agreeable here in Meryton," said Bingley, "Sir William Lucas is so hospitable and genteel, and you have also your Aunt and Uncle Philips, who love to give parties and gather the young people around them."

"My aunt and uncle are indeed invaluable in that way, and Charlotte Lucas has been like a sister to us," said Edward, "growing up with four brothers, I have missed the gentler company of a sister. You are most fortunate to have two sisters of your own."

"She seems like a very pleasant young woman," said Bingley.

At which juncture, a diversion came from a not wholly unexpected source.

As soon as the --shire had arrived in Meryton, Luke had struck up a friendship with Mrs Forster, wife of the Colonel of the Regiment, who looked on him quite as a younger brother. This invaluable friend was a very young woman, closer to Luke's age than to her husband's, and very lately married.

A passing resemblance between Luke and a much beloved younger brother left behind on her marriage, with the same good humour and good spirits she was missing, had recommended Luke to her. She was always ready to join in any of Luke's jokes, and Charles was invariably carried along behind them both.

An account of this joke is best related by Luke, to his mother after he and Charles were returned to   Longbourn by Colonel Forster's own carriage. John and Edward returned in their father's carriage in time for the second or third triumphant recital of their joke.

"Colonel Forster was out for the evening at that boring dinner, and Mrs Forster promised to have a little dance for us instead, and so she asked the two Harringtons to come, but Harriet was ill, and so Pen was forced to come by herself; and then, what do you think we did? We dressed up Chamberlayne in women's clothes, on purpose to pass for a lady – only think what fun! Not a soul knew it was Chamberlayne, not even Colonel Forster, only Mrs Forster and Charles and me, and my aunt, for we were forced to borrow one of her gowns, and you cannot imagine how well he looked. And then we took Chamberlayne along to the officers' dinner, and in he went, with us watching through the windows. When Denny and Pratt, and Colonel Forster and the others saw Chamberlayne, they did not know him in the least. Lord! How I laughed, when they all stood up when he came in, and they were all treating him like a lady! Mrs Forster was astonished how well Chamberlayne did at pretending to be a lady. I thought I should have died. And then the men suspected something, and Chamberlayne was found out, and they sent us home."

Edward and John were well accustomed to Luke's accounts of his parties and good jokes, but Edward had observed that Mr Darcy had regarded the unmasking of the fake lady with a steady, disapproving stare. Mr Bingley appeared to think it a most amusing jest, and Mr Hurst did not notice anything amiss at all, so focused was he on his drink and his food, and the promise of a game of cards after dinner.

Before being put into Colonel Forster's carriage, Luke spotted Mr Bingley in amongst the crowd of officers, and taxed him with having promised on his first coming into the country to give a ball at Netherfield.

Luke was a stout, well-grown boy of fifteen, with a fine complexion and good-humoured countenance; a favourite with his mother, whose affection extended well beyond any attempt to check his forward in public. He had high animal spirits, and a sort of natural self-consequence, which the company of the officers, to whom his uncle's good dinners and his own easy manners had recommended him, had increased into assurance. So he was utterly unabashed at being bundled into a carriage and sent home from the officers' dinner party, and was completely equal therefore to address Mr Bingley on the subject of the ball, and to abruptly remind him of his promise; adding, that it would be most shameful thing in the world if he did not keep it.

"I am perfectly ready, I assure you, to keep my engagement," was Bingley's courteous response, "and we will all be dancing soon at Netherfield."

Luke declared himself satisfied. "It would be much better to wait until Captain Carter was at Meryton again. And when you have given your ball, I shall insist on their giving one also. I shall tell Colonel Forster it will be quite a shame if he does not."

Colonel Forster gave the coachman his orders, and sent the two jokers home well satisfied with their evening's work.

Chapter Nine

The following day, Edward was astonished to be invited with John to a family dinner at Netherfield, for he had thought Luke and Charles's performance the night before would have given Mr Darcy at least a disgust of the Bennet family. But Netherfield was Mr Bingley's seat, not Mr Darcy's, and he could invite whomsoever he chose to dinner. Edward did wonder if it was at Miss Darcy's behest that the invitation was issued, and even if it were not, he welcomed the opportunity to spend more time in her company. John was equally hopeful that the invitation proceeded from Miss Bingley's desire to spend more time in his company.

"Well," Mrs Bennet was greatly gratified that they should be invited again so soon, "I cannot think why Mr Bingley does not invite us all, but you must go, John, and Edward, and bring us back a report of what they eat; I have not been able to get a bit of fish for two weeks now, but maybe Miss Bingley has more luck, or can send to town."

"We will do our best to satisfy your curiosity as to how the Bingleys dine, Mama," said Edward, as he and John went up to dress, "I also cannot understand why we are not all invited." In truth, he knew that Miss Bingley and Mrs Hurst did not approve of either his mother, nor his younger brothers.

At half past six, they arrived at Netherfield Hall for the dinner.

To the civil enquiries after the rest of his family, Edward made slight answer. During the meal itself he had very little notice from any but Mr Bingley and Miss Darcy, whose gentle attentions proved her to be more well bred than Miss Bingley, who addressed an occasional comment to John, or Mrs Hurst, but who talked almost exclusively to Mr Darcy and Mr Bingley, and all but ignored Edward. As for Mr Hurst, by whom Edward sat, he was an indolent man, who lived only to eat, drink and play at cards, and did not even recall they had met the previous evening at the officers' dinner.

When dinner was over and the gentlemen joined the ladies, Edward sat by Miss Darcy and picked up the book she had been reading. Mr Hurst looked at him with astonishment as he walked past to the card table.

"Do you prefer reading to cards?" said he, "That is rather singular."

"I have pleasure in many things," Edward replied, but Mr Hurst was already sitting down at the card table and did not hear.

"Mr Bennet," he called, "we are in need of a fourth at cards." John walked over to join him, casting a look back at Miss Bingley, which she did not notice, but Edward did, and it gave him pain. He feared that John was about to see that Miss Bingley was too much taken up with Mr Darcy to care for a mere Mr Bennet.

Mr Bingley said, "I wish my collection were larger for Miss Darcy's benefit and my own credit; but I am an idle fellow, and though I have not many, I have more than I ever look into."

Miss Darcy thanked him, and assured him that she could suit herself perfectly with the books available in the room.

"I am astonished," said Miss Bingley, sitting down on the other side of Miss Darcy, "that my father should have left so small a collection of books. What a delightful library you have at Pemberley, Mr Darcy."

"It ought to be good, ought not it, Fitzwilliam?" said Miss Darcy to her brother, "It has been the work of many generations of Darcys; and then we have added to it. We are always buying books." This last with a glance at Edward.

"I cannot comprehend the neglect of a family library in such days as these," said Mr Darcy with a fond smile at his sister.

"Neglect!" cried Miss Bingley, "I am sure you neglect nothing that can add to the beauties of that noble place. Charles, when you build your house, I wish it may be half as delightful as Pemberley."

"I wish it may."

"But I would really advise you to make your purchase in that neighbourhood, and take Pemberley for a kind of model. There is not a finer county in England than Derbyshire."

"With all my heart; I will buy Pemberley itself if Darcy would sell it."

"I am talking of possibilities, Charles."

"Upon my word, Caroline, I should think it more   possible to get Pemberley by purchase than imitation."

Mr Hurst called out to his sister to join the card players, which broke up this conversation. Miss Bingley walked over to the card table and as most of the party was now in that part of the room, Edward stood, offered Miss Darcy his arm and they walked over to the card table to station themselves between Mr Hurst and his sister, to better observe the game.

"How you are grown since the Spring," said Miss Bingley looking up at Miss Darcy. "You are nearly Mr Bennet's height. And you are so accomplished for your age! Your performance on the piano-forte is exquisite."

Edward smiled down at the top of Miss Darcy's head, but he could tell by her withdrawn face, that Miss Darcy did not like having attention drawn to her thus, and attempted to turn the conversation into a more general direction.

"It is amazing how young ladies have the patience to be so very accomplished as they all are."

Miss Bingley exclaimed,

"All young ladies accomplished? Whatever can you mean, Mr Bennet?"

It was her brother who took up the thought instead.

"I agree with Edward. They all paint tables, cover skreens and net purses. I scarcely heard of a young lady spoken of for the first time, without being informed that she was very accomplished."

This drew in Mr Darcy.

"Your list of the common extent of accomplishments," said he, "has too much truth. The word is applied to many a woman who deserves it no otherwise than by netting a purse, or covering a skreen. But I am very far from agreeing with you in your estimation of ladies in general. I cannot boast of knowing more than half a dozen, in the whole range of my acquaintance, that are really accomplished."

"Nor I, I am sure," said Miss Bingley.

"Then," observed Edward, "You must comprehend a great deal in your idea of an accomplished woman."

"Yes; I do comprehend a great deal in it."

"Oh! Certainly," cried his faithful assistant, "no one can be really esteemed accomplished, who does not greatly surpass what is usually met with. A woman must have a thorough knowledge of music, singing, drawing, dancing and all the modern languages, to deserve the word; and besides all this, she must possess a certain something in her air and manner of walking, the tone of her voice, her address and expressions, or the word will be but half-deserved."

"All this she must possess," added Darcy, "and to all this she must yet add something more substantial, in the improvement of her mind by extensive reading. This I have constantly recommended to Miss Darcy, and as Miss Bingley observes, she is much improved."

Miss Darcy turned away in embarrassment at having the company's attention drawn to her again, and Mr Hurst called them all to order, with bitter complaints of their inattention to the card table and the game going forward.

As the conversation was thereby at an end, Edward took this opportunity to draw near to Miss Darcy again and observe,

"Until I met you, Miss Darcy, I never saw a woman with such capacity, and taste, and application, and elegance united."

She blushingly disclaimed all pretence to such a list of accomplishments and their conversation continued to the great satisfaction of both, until the card game broke up, and the evening was over.

After John and Edward had made their bows and departed, Miss Bingley said, "Mr Edward Bennet's opinion of women is not high, perhaps he seeks to recommend himself to other gentlemen by undervaluing women. In my opinion, it is a paltry device, a very mean art."

"It may be so," replied Darcy, to whom this remark was chiefly addressed, "but there is a meanness in all the arts which gentlemen and ladies sometimes condescend to employ for captivation or approval. Whatever bears affinity to cunning is despicable."

Miss Bingley was not so entirely satisfied with this reply as to continue the subject.

On their way home, John said, "I saw you much in conversation with Miss Darcy."

"Yes," replied Edward, "we converse very easily; she is just the sort of woman who, in disposition, and talents, would most suit me. Her understanding, and temper, would answer all my wishes. But I cannot hope that Mr Darcy would look on any offer from me with any favour."

"Then you must tell him of your true circumstances," said John.

But Edward instead asked if John had managed any conversation with Miss Bingley.

"She was much in demand, and in a family party such as this, it was not possible," John replied, "But I shall hope to see her again soon." And as Edward listened to the happy, though modest hopes which John entertained of Miss Bingley's regard, he wondered that John had not noticed how engrossed Miss Bingley was with Mr Darcy, and turned the subject.

"Did you notice if there was fish?" asked he, "Mama is sure to ask, and I cannot recall!"

Chapter Ten

Had John been invited again the following evening, Miss Bingley's attentions towards Mr Darcy might have been obvious enough even for him to notice.

That evening after dinner, the Bingleys, Hursts and Darcys all collected again in the drawing room. Mr Hurst reminded his sister-in-law of the card-table - but in vain. She had obtained private intelligence that Mr Darcy did not wish for cards; and Mr Hurst soon found even his open petition rejected. She assured him that no one intended to play, and the silence of the whole party on the subject, seemed to justify her. Mr Hurst had therefore nothing to do, but to stretch himself on one of the sophas and go to sleep. Miss Darcy was seated at the piano-forte. Mr Darcy was writing, and Miss Bingley seated near him, was watching the progress of his letter, and calling off his attention by offering repeated suggestions and assistance.

The perpetual commendations of the lady on either Mr Darcy's handwriting, or on the evenness of his lines, or on the length of his letter, with the perfect unconcern with which these praises were received, formed a curious dialogue, and one to which the others in the room paid no heed.

"You write uncommonly fast."

"You are mistaken. I write rather slowly."

"How many letters you must have occasion to write in the course of the year! Letters of business, I expect. How odious I should think them!"

"It is fortunate, then, that they fall to my lot instead of to yours."

"I am afraid you do not like your pen. Let me mend it for you. I mend pens remarkably well."

"Thank you – but I always mend my own."

"How can you contrive to write so even?"

He was silent.

"It is a rule with me, that a person who can write a long letter, with ease, cannot write ill."

Mr Bingley looked up at last from his cards at this observation.

"That will not do for a compliment to Darcy, Caroline," he cried, "because he does not write with ease. He studies too much for words of four syllables. Do not you, Darcy?"

"My stile of writing is very different from yours."

"Oh!" cried Miss Bingley, "Charles writes in the most careless way imaginable, and I can scarcely make out a syllable for the blots and crossings."

"My ideas flow so rapidly that I have not time to express them – by which means my letters sometimes convey no ideas at all to my correspondents. It is a wonder to me that the Mr Bennets understood that my note was an invitation and came to the officers' dinner."

The mention of the Mr Bennets aroused Miss Darcy's attention and she closed the piano-forte lid and joined the party.

"Your humility, Mr Bingley," said she, "must disarm reproof."

"My dear sister," said Darcy, "nothing is more deceitful than the appearance of humility. It is often only carelessness of opinion, and sometimes an indirect boast."

"And which of the two do you call my little recent piece of modesty?"

"The indirect boast; for you are really proud of your defects in writing, because you consider them as proceeding from a rapidity of thought and a carelessness of execution, which if not estimable, you think at least highly interesting. The power of doing any thing with quickness is always much prized by the possessor, and often without any attention to the imperfection of the performance. When you told Mr Edward Bennet at the officers' dinner that if you ever resolved on quitting Netherfield you should be gone in five minutes, you meant it to be a sort of panegyric, of a compliment to yourself – and yet what is there so very laudable in a precipitance which must leave very necessary business undone, and can be of no real advantage to yourself or any one else?"

"Nay," cried Bingley, "It is too much to reveal much later all the foolish things that were said at a gentlemen's dinner! And yet, upon my honour, I believed what I said of myself to be true, and I believe it at this moment. At least, therefore, I did not assume the character of needless precipitance to show off before any ladies."

The reference to the officers' dinner and to ladies raised some less than congenial memories for Darcy, but he was certain that the ladies present could know nothing of it, and so he continued with the argument at hand.

"I dare say you believed it; but I am no means convinced that you would be gone with such celerity; your conduct would be quite as dependant on chance as that of any man I know; and if, as you were mounting your horse, a friend were to say, 'Bingley, you had better stay till next week,' you would probably do it, you would probably not go -and, at another word, might stay a month."

Miss Darcy took pity on Mr Bingley, and cried, "You have only proved by this, that Mr Bingley did not do justice to his own disposition. You have shewn him off now much more than he did himself."

"I am exceedingly gratified, Miss Darcy," said Bingley, "by your converting what your brother has said into a compliment on the sweetness of my temper. But I am afraid you are giving it a turn that Fitzwilliam did by no means intend; for he would certainly think the better of me, if under such a circumstance I were to give a flat denial, and ride off as fast as I could."

Miss Darcy laughed at such a picture, but could tell her brother was rather offended by the turn of the conversation, and Miss Bingley joined in at his defence too, and expostulated with her brother for talking such nonsense.

Mr Darcy finished his letter and applied to his sister and Miss Bingley for the indulgence of some music. Mrs Hurst turned the pages for Miss Darcy, and sang with her sister, and peace was restored to the family party, until Miss Bingley started to talk of the Bennet family with disapprobation concerning the inferiority of their connections.

"The mother," said she, "needs to be given some hints as to the advantage of holding her tongue, and from what I hear, the younger sons are forever running after the militia in Meryton. And their uncle Philips is nothing but a country attorney, for all that he gives endless noisy parties. I much prefer the elegance and quiet of our family evenings at home."

Darcy and Bingley exchanged a glance, hoping that Miss Bingley had not heard the details of the younger Bennets' incursion into the officers' dinner, and soon after every body retired for the night.

Chapter Eleven

"I hope, my dear," said Mr Bennet to his wife, as they were at breakfast the next morning, "that you have ordered a good dinner to-day, because I have reason to expect an addition to our family party."

"Who do you mean, my dear? I know of nobody that is coming I am sure, unless Charlotte Lucas should happen to call in, and I hope my dinners are good enough for her. I do not believe she often sees such at home."

"The person of whom I speak, is a gentleman, and one we have not seen nor heard from for many years."

Mrs Bennet cast her mind about to think of whom he could be referring. "Is it Mr Bingley? Well, I am sure I shall be extremely glad to see Mr Bingley. But – good lord! How unlucky! There is still not a bit of fish to be got to-day. Luke, my love, ring the bell. I must speak to Hill, this moment."

"It is not Mr Bingley," said her husband, "Attend that I said we had not seen this gentleman for many years, and we saw Mr Bingley but the other day."

This roused a general astonishment, and he had the pleasure of being eagerly questioned by his wife and five sons at once.

After amusing himself for some time with their curiosity, he thus explained. "About a month ago I received a letter, and about a fortnight ago I answered it, for I thought it a case of some delicacy, and requiring early attention. It is from Mr Collins, whom you may recall as a former tutor to our elder sons, and who retired from tutoring when faced with the prospect of our younger sons. I did not know where he went after he left here."

"I believe Mr Collins may have been at University," John said, "But it is a common enough name, and it may not be the same man."

"But why does he wish to return now?" said Mrs Bennet, "For

none of our sons have need of a tutor."

"On that score, I fear I must once again beg to differ with you, my dear," returned her husband, "for our youngest two sons are badly in want of   education. However, Mr Collins has moved on from tutoring unwilling young men, it seems, as you will hear."

Mr Bennet read out Mr Collins' letter to his family:

"Hunsford, near Westerham, Kent

15th October

Dear Sir,

I beg to bring myself to your attention after these many years have passed since I left your house. I have had the misfortune to lose my father, and since attaining to my majority, and completing my university education in the Divinities, I received Ordination at Easter this year. I have been so fortunate as to be distinguished by the patronage of the Right Honourable Lady Catherine de Bourgh, widow of Sir Lewis de Bourgh, whose bounty and beneficence has preferred me to the valuable

rectory of this parish, where it shall be my earnest endeavour to demean my-self with grateful respect   towards her Ladyship, and be ever ready to perform those rites and ceremonies which are instituted by the Church of England. As a clergyman, however, I feel it my duty to promote and establish the blessings of marriage in all families within the reach of my influence, and on these grounds I flatter myself that you would be willing to assist me to select a suitable bride from amongst your gently-bred acquaintance. I regret that I have no other father-figure to apply to for assistance, and always remember my time spent with your family as though I were quite one of your own sons. If you should have no objection to receive me into your house, I propose myself the satisfaction of waiting

upon you and your family, Monday November 18th, by four o'clock, and shall probably trespass on your hospitality until the Saturday se'enight following, which I can do without any inconvenience, as Lady Catherine is far from objecting to my occasional absence on a Sunday, provided that some other clergyman is engaged to do the duty of the day Moreover, her Ladyship herself has twice condescended to give me her opinion (unasked too!) on this subject; and has told me that a clergyman such as myself should marry. Prior to my arrival, if you would be so good as to cast your mind over the daughters of your acquaintance; I hope your sons have not already carried away the flowers of the country. As for specifications; her Ladyship requires a gentlewoman, for her sake, and an active, useful sort of person, not brought up high, but able to make a small income go a long way, for my sake. Should I be fortunate enough to encounter such a woman, and my suit with her should prosper, Lady Catherine has promised me that when I bring my bride to Hunsford, she will visit her. I remain, dear sir, with respectful compliments to your lady and sons, your well-wisher and friend, William Collins."

"At four o'clock, therefore, we may expect this amorously inclined gentleman to come amongst us once more," said Mr Bennet, folding up the letter, "He seems to have turned into a most conscientious and polite man, upon my word; and I doubt not will prove a valuable acquaintance, especially if Lady Catherine should be so indulgent as to let him come to us again, after he is married."

There was a short silence while all present considered the oddness of Mr Collins' request.

Edward was chiefly struck with his extraordinary   deference for Lady Catherine, and his kind intention of christening, marrying, and burying his parishioners whenever it was required.

"He must be an oddity, I think," said he, "I cannot make him out. There is something very pompous in his stile. And what can he mean about your suggesting   daughters of your acquaintance as his bride? Can he be a sensible man, sir?"

"No, my dear; I think not. I have great hopes of finding him quite the reverse. There is a mixture of servility and self-importance in his letter, which promises well. I am impatient to see him."

"In point of composition," said Mark, "his letter does not seem defective. I remember well our studies on   Cicero, and the rhetorical stile."

Mr Bennet rose and bowed to his wife, "If you will excuse me my dear, I must write to all our acquaintance to ask them to line up their marriageable daughters for Mr Collins' inspection. Do you suppose Abbot might be released in order to deliver the letters?"

To this Mrs Bennet replied, "Oh! I cannot think him serious, Mr Bennet, it is not at all the thing. What a pity we did not have a daughter; he could have married her!"

To Charles and Luke, neither the letter nor its writer was in any degree interesting. They had both declined lessons from Mr Collins, and in Luke's case, behaved so badly to any body engaged to tutor him, that Mr Bennet withdrew funding, and his two youngest sons were left to shift for themselves. Determined to be lazy and ignorant, they had carried their point. It was next to impossible that their former tutor should come in a scarlet coat, and it was now some weeks since they had received any pleasure or paid any attention to any body but men in that colour. As for Mrs Bennet, she was puzzled as to Mr Collins' reasons for his visit, but was preparing to see him with a degree of composure, which astonished her husband and sons. Now that she knew him to be a man of lesser degree than Mr Bingley, it mattered not whether there was any fish to be had, but she was still resolved to be-speak a very fine family dinner to impress a man whose patron was a Lady Catherine de Bourgh.

Mr Collins was punctual to his time, and was received with great politeness by the whole family. John,   Edward and Mark indeed had a debt of gratitude to Mr Collins for the learning they had received at his desk, which had enabled John to go on to University, and Mark to the Grammar School. Mr Collins himself had matured into a tall, heavy looking man of five and thirty. His air was grave and stately, and his manners were very formal. Of all of them, he seemed the most aware of his previously dependent situation, and of what he considered now to be his much-elevated   position, which gave his discourse a sonorous, soporific quality.

His lengthy description of the minutiae of his journey from Hunsford to Longbourn was interrupted by a summons to dinner, and he offered Mrs Bennet his arm to lead her into the dining room, with a bow that would not have looked out of place at Sir William Lucas's presentation at St James's palace. He ate and praised with delighted alacrity, and looked as if he felt that life could furnishing nothing greater. Mrs Bennet was gratified by this excessive admiration, although she did wonder whether he was drawing a comparison to the much plainer fare he had been served in his own room when he was her sons' tutor.

Chapter Twelve

During dinner, Mr Bennet scarcely spoke at all; but when the servants were withdrawn, he thought it time to reacquaint himself with his surprising guest, and therefore started a subject in which he expected him to shine, by observing that he seemed very fortunate in his patroness.

Lady Catherine de Bourgh's attention to his wishes, and consideration for his comfort, appeared very remarkable. Mr Bennet could not have chosen better. Mr Collins was eloquent in her praise. The subject elevated him to more than usual solemnity of manner, and with a most important aspect he protested that he had never in his life witnessed such behaviour in a person of rank – it seemed clear that he did not count Mr Bennet in that exalted company – such affability and condescension, as he had himself experienced from Lady Catherine. She had been graciously pleased to approve of both the discourses, which he had already had the honour of preaching before her. She had also asked him twice to dine at Rosings, and had sent for him only the Saturday before, to make up her pool of quadrille in the evening. Lady Catherine was reckoned proud by many people he knew, but he had never seen any thing but affability in her. She had always spoken to him as she would to any other gentleman; she made not the smallest objection to his joining in the society of the neighbourhood, nor to his leaving his parish occasionally for a week or two, to visit friends such as the Bennets; at least, he flattered himself that he could count the family as his friends. She had even condescended to advise him to marry as soon as he could, provided he chose with discretion (and here Mr Collins nodded towards Mr Bennet as though to remind him of his own duty in locating a suitable bride); and had once paid him a visit in his humble parsonage; where she had perfectly approved all the alterations he had been making, and had even vouchsafed to suggest some herself, - some shelves in the closets upstairs.

"That is all very proper and civil, I am sure," said Mrs Bennet, "and I dare say she is a very agreeable woman. It is a pity that great ladies and gentlemen in general are not more like her. Does she live near you, sir?"

"The garden in which stands my humble abode, is separated only by a lane from Rosings Park, her ladyship's residence."

"I think you said she was a widow, sir? Has she any family?"

"She has only one daughter, the heiress of Rosings, and of very extensive property."

"Ah!" cried Mrs Bennet, with significant looks both at Mr Bennet and at John, "Then she would be a valuable addition to any family. And what sort of young lady is she? Is she handsome? You can see how well John has grown-up; he is very handsome, and not yet wed."

Mr Collins bowed towards John, but would not be diverted into machinations towards any body else's marriage plans. "She is a most charming young lady indeed. Lady Catherine herself says that in point of true beauty, Miss de Bourgh is far superior to the

handsomest of her sex; because there is that in her features which marks the young woman of distinguished birth. Lady Catherine advised me not to look for those marks in my future wife, as that would be raising my eyes too high. Miss de Bourgh is unfortunately of a sickly constitution, which has prevented her making that progress in many accomplishments, which she could not otherwise have failed of; as I am informed by the lady who superintended her education, and who still resides with them. But she is perfectly amiable, and often condescends to drive by my humble abode in her phaeton and ponies."

"Has she been presented? I do not remember her name among the ladies at court."

"Her indifferent state of health unhappily prevents her being in town; and by that means, as I told Lady Catherine myself one day, has deprived the British court of its brightest ornament. Her ladyship seemed pleased with the idea, and you may imagine that I am happy on every occasion to offer those little delicate compliments which are always acceptable to ladies. I have more than once observed to Lady Catherine, that her charming daughter seemed born to be a duchess, and that the most elevated rank, instead of giving her consequence, could be adorned by her. These are the kind of little things which please her ladyship, and it is a sort of attention which I conceive myself peculiarly bound to pay."

"You judge very properly," said Mr Bennet, "and it is happy for you that you possess the talent of flattering with delicacy. Your future wife will be a lucky woman indeed, if you vouchsafe her a share of these   compliments. May I ask whether these pleasing attentions proceed from the impulse of the moment, or are the result of previous study?"

"They arise chiefly from what is passing at the time, and though I sometimes amuse myself with suggesting and arranging such little elegant compliments as may be adapted to ordinary occasions, I always wish to give them as unstudied an air as possible."

Mr Bennet's expectations were fully answered. His sons' former tutor had not been improved by the years away from the Bennet household; instead he had become absurd. Mr Bennet listened to Mr Collins with the keenest enjoyment, maintaining at the same time the most resolute composure of countenance, and except in an occasional glance at Edward, requiring no partner in his pleasure.

By tea-time, however the dose had been enough, and Mr Bennet was glad to take his guest into the drawing-room again, and when tea was over, glad to invite him to read aloud. Mr Collins readily assented, and a book was produced; but on beholding it, (for every thing announced it to be from a lending library) he started back, and begging pardon, protested that he never read novels. Mark hurried to provide more suitable books, and after some deliberation, Mr Collins chose Fordyce's Sermons. Luke gaped as Mr Collins opened the volume, and before he had, with very monotonous solemnity, read three pages, he interrupted him with,

"Do you know, mama, that my uncle Philips talks of turning away Richard, and if he does, Colonel Forster will hire him. My aunt told me so herself on Saturday. I shall walk to Meryton tomorrow to hear mor about it, and to ask when Mr Denny comes back from town."

Mark was astonished by this as it had not been mentioned by his uncle, during their working hours; but before he could question Luke further, both were bid by their two eldest brothers to hold his tongue; and Mr Collins, much offended, laid aside the book and said,

"It appears that the years passing have not improved the youngest gentleman's interest in books of a serious stamp, though written solely for his benefit, and would greatly assist in regulating their behaviour in company. It amazes me, I confess, for certainly there can be nothing more advantageous to him as instruction. But I will no longer importune the younger gentleman."

Then turning to Mr Bennet, he offered himself as his antagonist at backgammon. Mr Bennet referred Mr Collins to John, who was an adept at backgammon, contenting himself instead with observing that Mr Collins acted very wisely in leaving the youngest boys to their own trifling amusements. Mark apologised most civilly for Luke's interruption, and promised it should not occur again, if Mr Collins would resume his book; but Mr Collins after assuring them all that he bore his former pupil no ill will, and should never resent his behaviour as any affront, seated himself at the backgammon table with John, turning his back on Luke.

Chapter Thirteen

Mr Collins had not grown into a sensible man, and the deficiency of nature had been but little assisted either by his education nor by the society he had mixed with. The greatest part of his life had been spent under the guidance of an illiterate and miserly father, who had not understood his son's desire to better himself through education, and had forced the young Mr Collins to go out as a tutor to gentlemen's sons. After his father's death, he had attended university, kept all the necessary terms, and crammed his head with as much learning as possible, without any of the attendant understanding necessary to turn the lessons into something profound, or bettering. He had not formed any useful acquaintance at university, not being a gentleman's son, and not having any thing about him which attracted him to other men as a friend, acquaintance, or to offer him any useful patronage. The subjection in which his father had brought him up had given him originally great humility of manner, which was useful when living in the households of his employers, and it had been at this stage of his life that he had taught the elder three Bennet boys the basics they would need as gentlemen and scholars.

But this natural humility had been now a good deal counteracted by the self-conceit of a weak head, living in retirement after quitting university, and the consequential feelings of early and unexpected prosperity. A fortunate chance had recommended him to Lady Catherine de Bourgh when the living of Hunsford was vacant; and the respect which he felt for her high rank, and his veneration for her as his patroness, mingling with a very good opinion of himself, of his authority as a clergyman, and his rights as a rector, made him altogether a mixture of pride and obsequiousness, self-importance, and humility.

Having now a good house and a very sufficient income, he intended to marry, and in seeking out his former employer, he hoped to be introduced to the cream of Meryton society, and to take his choice amongst their daughters. As he had met with more kindness at the Bennet house as a much younger man than had ever been on offer at home, they were his first choice for a location in which to further his plans – he had no other friends, and Hunsford parish could furnish no lady to the exact requirements of Lady Catherine.

Luke's intention of walking to Meryton was not forgotten; every one except Mark agreed to go with him; and Mr Collins was to attend them, at the request of Mr Bennet, who was most anxious to get rid of him, and have his library to himself; for thither Mr Collins and Mark had followed him after breakfast, and there they would continue, nominally engaged with the many volumes there to be found, but really Mr Collins could not be kept focused on helping Mark through a difficult passage of Cicero. Instead, he talked with little cessation, of his house and garden at Hunsford. In some ways this was to deter Mark from attempting to draw him back in as an unpaid tutor, but also because he wanted Mr Bennet to acknowledge how far he had progressed since he was last at Longbourn.

Such doings had discomposed Mr Bennet exceedingly. In his library he had always been sure of leisure and tranquillity; and though prepared, as he told Edward, to meet with folly and conceit in every other room in the house, he was used to be free from them there; his civility, therefore, was most prompt in inviting Mr Collins to join the young gentlemen on their walk; and leave the elder to his private contemplations. Mr Collins saw this as an opportunity to be introduced to the principal families of Meryton, and being much better fitted for a walker than a reader, was extremely pleased to walk away from the large book that Mark had just opened invitingly, and go.

In pompous nothings on his side, and civil assents on that of his former pupils, their time passed till they entered Meryton. The attention of the younger ones was then no longer gained by him. Their eyes were immediately wandering up in the street in quest of the officers, and nothing less than a red coat could recall them.

Every body's attention was soon caught by a young man, whom they had never seen before, of most gentlemanlike appearance, walking with an officer on the other side of the way. The officer was the very Mr Denny, concerning whose return from London Luke came to enquire. All were struck with the stranger's air, and wondered who he could be; Luke, presuming on his youth, high spirits, and former acquaintance with Mr Denny, crossed immediately and demanded to be introduced.

The others followed Luke across, and Mr Denny introduced his friend, Mr Wickham, who had returned with him the day before from town, and he was happy to say had accepted a commission in their corps.

This was exactly as it should be; for the young man wanted only regimentals to make him completely charming, and another candidate for the adulation of the youngest Bennet boys. His appearance was greatly in his favour; he had all the best part of beauty, a fine countenance, a good figure, and very pleasing address. The introduction was followed up on his side by a happy readiness of conversation – a readiness at the same time perfectly correct and unassuming; and the whole party were still standing and talking together very agreeably, when the sound of horses drew their notice, and Darcy and Bingley were seen riding down the street.

On distinguishing the elder Bennets in the group, the two gentlemen came directly towards them, and began the usual civilities. Mr Bingley was then, he said, on his way to Longbourn to pay his respects to their mother, and replied to John's enquiries after Miss Bingley and the Hursts. Edward happened to be looking at Mr Darcy, wondering if he might enquire about Miss Darcy, when the latter appeared to notice one of the strangers in their midst. Mr Collins was of no interest to him, but the other had the most extraordinary effect. The countenance of both as they looked at each other, was all astonishment at this meeting: both changed colour, one looked white, the other red. Mr Wickham after a few moments, touched his hat – a salutation which Mr Darcy just deigned to return. What could be the meaning of it? It was impossible to imagine; it was not to long to know.

In another minute Mr Bingley, but without seeming to have noticed what passed, took his leave of John, and rode on with his friend.

Mr Denny and Mr Wickham walked with the Bennets and Mr Collins to the door of Mr Philips' house, and then made their bows, in spite of Luke's pressing entreaties that they would come in, and even in spite of Mrs Philips' throwing up the parlour window and loudly seconding the invitation.

Mrs Philips was always glad to see her nephews, not being blessed with children of her own. Mark she saw whenever he was with Mr Philips at the office, but she found the others more lively company. She knew about the arrival of the new officer, because she happened to see Mr Jones's shop boy in the street, who told her about the orders newly flowing from the returning Mr Denny; when her civility was claimed towards Mr Collins by John's introduction of him. She received him with her very best politeness, which he returned with as much more, apologising for his intrusion, without any previous acquaintance with her, which he could not help flattering himself however might be justified by his being a guest of the young gentleman who intro- duced him to her notice.

Mrs Philips was quite awed by such excess of good breeding; but her contemplation of one stranger was soon put to an end by exclamations and enquiries about the other, of whom however, she could only relate what they already knew; that Mr Denny had brought him from London, that he was to have a lieuten- ant's commission in the -shire. She had been watching him the last hour, she said, as he walked up and down the street.

The officers were to dine with Mr Philips the next day, and Mrs Philips promised to make her husband call on Mr Wickham, and give him an invitation also, if the family from Longbourn would come in the evening. This was agreed to, and Mrs Philips pro- tested that they would have a nice comfortable noisy game of lottery tickets, and a little bit of hot supper afterwards. The prospect of such delights was very cheering, and they parted in mutual good spirits. Mr Collins repeated his apologies in quit- ting the room, and was assured with unceasing civility that they were perfectly needless.

As they walked home, Edward related to John what he had seen pass between the two gentlemen; but though John would have defended either or both, had they appeared to be wrong, he could no more explain such behaviour than his brother.

Mr Collins on his return highly gratified Mrs Bennet by admiring Mrs Philips's manners and politeness. He protested that except Lady Catherine and her daughter; he had never seen a more elegant woman; for she had not only received him with the utmost civility, but had even pointedly included him in her invitation for the next evening, although utterly unknown to her before. Something he supposed might be attributed to his long connection with them, but yet he had never met with so much attention in the whole course of his life.

Chapter Fourteen

As no objection was made to the young people's engagement with their aunt, and all Mr Collins's scruples about leaving Mr and Mrs Bennet for a single evening during his visit were most steadily resisted, the coach conveyed him and the five Bennet boys at a suitable hour to Meryton; and they had the pleasure of hearing, as they entered the drawing room, that Mr Wickham had accepted their uncle's invitation, and was then in the house.

When this information was given, and they had all taken their seats, Mr Collins was at leisure to look around him and admire, and he was so much struck with the size and furniture of the apartment, that declared he could almost have supposed himself in the small summer breakfast parlour at Rosings; a comparison that did not at first convey much gratification, but when Mrs Philips understood from him what Rosings was, and who was its proprietor, when she had listened to the description of only one of Lady Catherine's drawing-rooms, and found that the chimney pieces alone had cost eight hundred pounds, she felt all the force of the compliment, and would hardly have resented a comparison with the housekeeper's room.

In describing to her all the grandeur of Lad Catherine and her mansion, with occasional digressions in praise of his own humble abode, in case Mrs Philips might have some eligible young ladies at hand who would pass Lady Catherine's scrutiny, he was happily employed until the gentlemen joined them; and he found in Mrs Philips a most attentive listener, whose opinion of his consequence increased with what she heard, and who was resolving to retail it all among her neighbours as soon as she could. Unfortunately for Mr Collins, it did not occur to Mrs Philips that he might be in want of a wife who could appreciate all the improvements he was making to his humble parsonage, and she had no daughter to dispose of in this manner; so all Mr Collins's hints were wasted.

The gentlemen approached, and Mr Wickham walked in amongst the officers, who presented a much superior countenance, air and walk to the broad-faced, stuffy uncle Philips, breathing port wine, who followed them into the room. John was already conversing with Maria Lucas, and so it was Edward that Mr Wickham recognised first, and he walked across to seat himself beside Edward where he immediately fell into agreeable conversation, though it was only on its being a wet night, and on the probability of the rainy season to come. This, contrasted with the dullness of the   conversation prior to his entrance, made Edward very aware of the very great pleasure a good speaker could give; for the commonest, dullest, most threadbare topic might be thus rendered interesting; it appeared that not only was Mr Wickham handsome, but of uncommon intelligence and verbal skill.

The ladies present, with the exception of Mrs Philips, gravitated towards the officers, and the   Bennets, and Mr Collins seemed likely to sink into   insignificance, despite frequently turning his eyes towards the Lucases, the Harrises, and the Harringtons; he had not been introduced to them, but marked them down as possibilities in his matrimonial quest; there was time enough yet. For now, he had in Mrs Philips a kind listener and was, by her watchfulness, most abundantly supplied with coffee and muffin.

When the card tables were placed, he had an opportunity of obliging her in return, by sitting down to whist.

"I know little of the game at present," said he, "but I shall be glad to improve myself, for in my situation of life –" Mrs Philips was very thankful for his compliance, but could not wait for his reason.

Mr Wickham did not play at whist and so he and Edward moved away from Luke, who was a most determined talker, and had nearly engrossed him entirely in his determination to be every militia man's best friend. Fortunately, Luke was also extremely fond of lottery tickets, and he soon grew too much interested in the game, too eager in making bets and exclaiming after prizes, to have attention for anyone in particular, except for those playing as well.

Mr Wickham and Edward were therefore able to continue their talk, and Edward hoped that Mr Wickham might tell the history of his acquaintance with Mr Darcy, and explain why meeting in the street had caused such reaction from both gentlemen. Of course, on such short acquaintance, it could hardly be expected, but to Edward's surprise, Mr Wickham began the subject almost immediately. He inquired how far Netherfield was from Meryton; and then, in a more hesitating manner, how long Mr Darcy had been staying there.

"About a month," said Edward; and then, unwilling to let the subject drop, added, "He is a man of very large property in Derbyshire, I understand."

"Yes," replied Wickham, "his estate there is a noble one. A clear ten thousand per annum. You could not have met with a person more capable of giving you certain information on that head than myself – for I have been connected with his familiar in a particular manner from my infancy."

Edward could not but look surprised.

"You may well be surprised, Mr Bennet, at such an assertion, after seeing, as you probably might, the cold manner of our meeting yesterday. Are you much   acquainted with Mr Darcy?"

"No, not much," said Edward, "I have spent a few   evenings with the whole party, including one at their home; but I have not found Mr Darcy particularly agreeable."

"I have no right to give my opinion," said Wickham, "as to his being agreeable or otherwise. I am not qualified to form one. I have known him too long and too well to be a fair judge. It is impossible for me to be impartial. But I believe your opinion would surprize, and perhaps you would not express it thus any-where else? Here you are in your own family."

"Upon my word, I say no more here than I might say in any house in the neighbourhood, except Netherfield. Mr Darcy has not put himself out to be agreeable to any body except his family and friends at Netherfield. You will not find him more favourably spoken of by any one."

"I cannot pretend to be sorry," said Wickham, "that he or any man should not be estimated beyond their   deserts; but with him I believe it does not often happen. The world is blinded by his fortune and consequence, or frightened by his high and im-posing manners, and sees him only as he chuses to be seen."

"I should take him, even on my slight acquaintance, to be an ill-tempered man."

Wickham only shook his head. "I wonder if he is likely to be in this country much longer?"

"I do not at all know; but I have heard nothing of his going away, although he must have responsibilities to return to on his own estate, for all he stays on   Mr Bingley's. But I hope your plans in favour of the -shire will not be affected by his being in the neighbourhood."

"Oh! No – it is not for me to be driven away by Mr Darcy. If he wishes to avoid seeing me, he must go. We are not on friendly terms, and it always gives me pain to meet him, but I have no reason for avoiding him but what I might proclaim to all the world; a sense of very great ill-usage, and painful regrets at his being what he is. His father, the late Mr Darcy, was one of the best men that ever breathed, and the truest friend I ever had; and I can never be in company with this Mr Darcy without being grieved to the soul by a thousand tender recollections. His behaviour to myself has been scandalous; but I verily believe I could forgive him any thing and every thing, rather than his disappointing the hopes and disgracing the memory of his father."

Edward found the interest of the subject increase, and listened with very great attention, but the confidential nature of it prevented further inquiry.

Mr Wickham began to speak on more general topics, Meryton, the neighbourhood, the society, appearing highly pleased with all that he had yet seen. "It was the prospect of constant society, and good society which was my chief inducement to enter the - shire," he added, "I knew it to be a most respectable, agreeable corps, and my friend Denny tempted me farther by his accounts of their present quarters, and the very great attentions and excellent acquaintance Meryton had procured them. I have been a disappointed man, and my spirits will not bear solitude. I must have employment and society. A military life is not what I was intended for, but circumstances have now made it eligible. The church ought to have been my profession; I was brought up for the church, and I should at this time have been in possession of a most valuable living, had it pleased the gentleman we were speaking of just now."

"Indeed!"

"Yes – the late Mr Darcy bequeathed me the next presentation of the best living in his gift. He was my godfather, and excessively attached to me. I cannot do justice to his kindness. He meant to provide for me amply, and thought he had done it; but when the living fell, it was given elsewhere."

"I am shocked indeed," cried Edward, "but how could that be? How could his Will have been disregarded? Did you not seek legal redress? My uncle Philips –"

Wickham shook his head, "I have discussed it with many attorneys; and there was just such an informality in the terms of the bequest as to give me no hope from the law. A man of honour could not have doubted the intention; but Mr Darcy chose to doubt it – to treat it as merely conditional recommendation, and to assert that I had forfeited all claim to it by extravagance, imprudence, in short any thing or nothing.

Certain it is, that when the living became vacant two years ago, exactly as I was of an age to hold it, and that it was given to another man; and no less certain is it, that I cannot accuse myself of having really done any thing to deserve to lose it. I have a warm, unguarded temper, and I may have perhaps sometimes spoken my   opinion of him, and to him, too freely. I can recall nothing worse. But the fact is, that we are very   different sort of men, and that he hates me."

"This is quite shocking! He deserves to be publicly   disgraced."

"Some time or other he will be – but it shall not be by me. Till I can forget his father, I can never defy or   expose him."

"I honour you for such feelings," said Edward. "But what can have been his motive? What can have induced him to behave so cruelly? To treat in such a manner the godson, the friend, the favourite of his father! And one too, who had probably been his own companion from childhood, connected together, as I think you said, in the closest manner!"

"We were born in the same parish, within the same park, the greatest part of our youth was passed together; inmates of the same house, sharing the same amusements, objects of the same parental care. My father began life in the profession which your uncle, Mr Philips, appears to do so much credit to – but he gave up every thing to be of use to the late Mr Darcy, and devoted all his time to the care of the Pemberley property. He was most highly esteemed by Mr Darcy, a most intimate confidential friend. Mr Darcy often acknowledge himself to be under the greatest obligations to my father's active superintendence, and when immediately before my father's death, Mr Darcy gave him a voluntary promise of providing for me, I am convinced that he felt it to be as much a debt of gratitude to him, as of affection to myself."

"How strange!" cried Edward, "How abominable! I wonder that the very pride of this Mr Darcy has not made him just to you! If from no better motive, that he should not have been too proud to be dishonest – for dishonesty I must call it."

"It is wonderful," replied Mr Wickham, "for almost all his actions may be traced to pride; - and pride has often been his best friend. It has connected him nearer with virtue than any other feeling. We are none of us consistent; and in his behaviour to me, there were stronger impulses even than pride."

"I must confess I have noticed his disdain for those he considers beneath him, which includes myself. I have only been invited at the behest of Mr Bingley or Miss Darcy."

"Miss Darcy is here?" Wickham appeared astonished, "I had not known. Mr Darcy is a very kind and careful guardian of his sister, and you will generally hear him cried up as the most attentive and best of brothers."

"I consider his attentiveness and care somewhat over heavy-handed," said Edward, and related what Miss Darcy had told him about her attendance at parties, and not being allowed to stand up with anyone but her own party, at assemblies.

"That is indeed a shame," said Wickham, "as a child she was affectionate and pleasing, and extremely fond of me. I have devoted hours and hours to her amusement; but she is nothing to me now. Despite that, I am sorry indeed to hear that Mr Darcy is limiting her pleasures thus."

After this the talk became more general, and there were pauses and trials of other subjects. But Edward could not help reverting once more to the first, and saying,

"I am astonished at his intimacy with Mr Bingley! How can Mr Bingley, who seems good humour itself, and is, I really believe, truly amiable, be in friendship with such a man? How can they suit each other? Do you know Mr Bingley?"

"Not at all, but Mr Darcy can please where he chuses. He does not want abilities. He can be a conversible companion if he thinks it worth his while. Among those who are at all his equals in consequence, he is a very different man from what he is to the less prosperous."

Edward recalled to mind his evening spent with the Darcys, Bingleys and Hursts, and could not help agreeing that Mr Darcy had not been as amiable as Mr Bingley, nor as attentive to a guest's amusement as his sister.

The whist party soon afterwards breaking up, the players gathered around the other table, and Mr Collins took his station likewise. The usual inquiries as to his success were made by Edward, but it had not been very great; he had lost every point. Mrs Philips began to express her concern thereupon, he assured her with much earnest gravity that it was not of the least importance, that he considered the money as a mere trifle, and begged she would not make herself uneasy.

"I know very well, madam," said he, "that when persons sit down to a card table, they must take their chance of these things, and happily I am not in such circumstances as to make five shillings any object." Here he paused to look around the circle, and to direct the next remark towards the young women present. "There are undoubtedly many who could not say the same, but thanks to Lady Catherine de Bourgh, I am removed far beyond the necessity of regarding little matters."

Edward, stifling a laugh at this overt boast, noticed nevertheless that Mr Collins had caught Charlotte Lucas's attention, and that she was looking at him with a steady regard. But before he could make any move to turn her attention away, Mr Wickham was speaking again in a low voice, and asking whether Mr Collins were intimately acquainted with the family of De Bourgh.

"Lady Catherine," Edward replied, "has very lately given him a living. I hardly know how Mr Collins was first introduced to her notice, but he certainly has not known her long."

"You know, of course, that Lady Catherine and Lady Anne Darcy were sisters?"

"Then she is Mr Darcy's aunt?"

"Indeed. Her daughter, Miss De Bourgh, will have a very large fortune, and it is hoped that she and her cousin with unite the two estates."

This information made Edward smile, as he thought of poor Miss Bingley's valiant attempts to engage Mr Darcy's attentions to herself by lavishing affection on his sister and praise on himself, if he were already self-destined to another.

"Mr Collins," he contented himself with observing out loud to Mr Wickham, "speaks highly both of Lady   Catherine and her daughter; but I suspect his gratitude for her singling him out has misled him, and that she is an arrogant, conceited woman."

"I believe her to be both in a very great degree," replied Wickham; "I have not seen her for many years, but I very well remember that I never liked her, and that her manners were dictatorial and insolent."

Edward and Mr Wickham continued talking together till supper put an end to cards; and gave the ladies their share of Mr Wickham's attentions; even Charlotte Lucas, Edward was pleased to see, was in the admiring circle of women about the new officer. There could be no more opportunity for confidential conversation in the noise of Mrs Philips's supper party, but it was clear that Mr Wickham's manners recommended him to every body. Whatever he said, was said well; and whatever he did, done gracefully. As for Edward, he felt he had made a new, and valuable friend, and was very pleased with the outcome of the evening.

On the way home neither Luke nor Mr Collins were once silent. Luke talked incessantly of lottery tickets, of the fish he had lost, and the fish he had won, and Mr Collins in describing the civility of Mr and Mrs Philips, protesting that he did not in the least regard his losses at whist, enumerating all the dishes at supper, and   admiring all the young women who had been present, had more to say than he could well manage before the carriage stopped at Longbourn House.

Chapter Fifteen

Edward related to John the next day, what had passed between Mr Wickham and himself. John listened with astonishment and concern; he knew not how to believe that Mr Darcy could be so unworthy of Mr Bingley's regard and yet, it was not in his nature to question the veracity of a young man of such amiable appearance as Wickham. The possibility of his having really endured such unkindness, was enough to interest all his strongest feelings, and nothing therefore remained to be done, but to think well of them both, to defend the   conduct of each, and throw into the account of accident or mistake, whatever could not be otherwise explained.

"They have both," said he, "been deceived, I dare say, in some way or other, of which we can form no idea. Interested people have perhaps misrepresented each to the other. It is, in short, impossible for us to conjecture the causes or circumstances which may have alienated them, without actual blame on either side. When you go to your new estate, if I mistake not, it borders on Mr Darcy's?" Edward nodded, "then you will be with people who will know the whole story, and it may be that Mr and Mrs Fellowes can throw some light on the situation between these two gentlemen."

"Indeed, you may be correct, although being in the country, there may well be the interested parties of whom you speak, and the story Wickham related will be shown to be true."

"But do consider in what a disgraceful light it places Mr Darcy, to be treating his father's favourite in such a manner, one whom his father had promised to provide for. It is impossible. No man of common humanity, no man who had any value for his character, could be capable of it. Consider if our father had such a dependent on whom he placed a promise of future aid, I would honour that promise when I succeeded to the estate, regardless of the cost to myself, and so will you when you succeed to Mr Fellowes's estate."

When Edward and John returned into the house from the shrubbery where this conversation passed, it was to find they had just missed seeing some of the people of whom they were speaking; Mr Bingley and his sisters had called to give their personal invitation for the long expected ball at Netherfield, which was fixed for the following Tuesday. Miss Bingley and Mrs Hurst had staid so little a time, rising from their seats with an activity which took their brother by surprise, and hurried off as if eager to escape from Mrs Bennet's civilities.

There was also a letter for Edward from Mr and Mrs Fellowes, lamenting his long absence, understanding his wish to spend time with his family, but requesting his presence as soon as possible at his new home in the north country; he was to give them a date to send their carriage to bring him home.

The prospect of a ball was extremely agreeable to every body; although the loss of Edward was far less so, particularly to Mr Bennet.

"Of course, you must go," said he, looking at the letter, which Edward had given him to read, "Mr and Mrs Fellowes have been most indulgent to allow us this time with you, but they must now be your priority and you must go to them."

"Not until after the ball, my dear Mr Bennet," his lady cried, "it is being given in compliment to us, and Edward must be there or Mr Bingley will be slighted. Indeed, it is not to be thought of that Edward should go until after the ball, and if Mr and Mrs Fellowes will but wait a short while longer, my brother and sister are to visit us for Christmas. Mr Bingley came himself to give us the invitation, when he could have sent a servant with a card."

"I will write to Mr and Mrs Fellowes, mama," said Edward, "and request leave to stay for the ball, but I must give them a date to send their carriage soon afterwards."

Each member of the family, including Mr Collins, anticipated a different pleasure to be had on the occasion of a ball. John was hoping Miss Bingley would dance two dances with him again, and Edward was equally hopeful that, under her brother's watchful eye, Miss Darcy might be permitted to stand up with him. The happiness anticipated by Charles and Luke depended less on any single event, or any particular person; they were always eager to attend any lively and sociable occasion. Even Mark could assure his family that he had no disinclination for it.

"While I can have some leisure time to study all other evenings," said he, "it is enough. I think it no sacrifice to join occasionally in evening entertainments. Society has claims on us all, and I know my uncle Philips would wish me to keep a presence in the local drawing rooms, and ball rooms, where clients may be found. I profess myself also as one of those who consider intervals of recreation and amusement as desirable for every body."

For Mr Collins, it was the opening he had been looking for to begin his campaign proper; for at a ball, it is easy to be introduced to a wide range of people, and there would surely be many young ladies there worthy of   becoming the mistress of Hunsford Parsonage, and for whom life could offer no greater pleasure than that of assisting to form a quadrille table at Rosings, in the   absence of more eligible visitors.

If there had not been a Netherfield ball to prepare for, and talk of, the younger Master Bennets would have been in a pitiable state at this time, for from the day of the invitation, to the day of the ball, there was such a succession of rain as prevented their walking into Meryton once. No aunt, no officers, no news could be sought after. They even took to questioning Mark on his return from his uncle Philips's office, but he could not, or would not, satisfy their curiosity. Nothing less than a dance on Tuesday, could have made such a Friday, Saturday, Sunday and Monday, endurable to Charles and Luke.

Mr Collins too was impatient with the weather, for no body called at the house, and the Bennets were not   engaged any where else either. Time was running short for his campaign, and almost no progress had been made to secure him a suitable bride.

Chapter Sixteen

Till the Bennets entered the drawing-room at Netherfield and looked at the cluster of red coats, it had not occurred to any of them that Mr Wickham would not be there after his brave declaration at Mrs Philips's party. It had also not occurred to Edward that Miss Darcy would not be there; he had not heard that she was gone, but so it seemed. He had dressed with more than usual care, and prepared in the highest spirits for the conquest of all that remained unsubdued of Miss Darcy's heart, trusting that it was not more that might be won in the course of the evening.

Had Edward been able to carry out this plan, he intended next to go to her brother, and to acquaint him with the truth of his own circumstances. But in an instant arose the dreadful suspicion of Mr Darcy having removed his sister from the neighbourhood in order to prevent her clear preference for a young man from what he would consider a most undeserving family.

Information needed to be sought about both noticeable absences, and it was Wickham's friend, Denny, to whom Luke eagerly applied, and who told them that Wickham had been obliged to go to town on business the day before, and was not yet returned; adding, with a significant smile,

"I do not imagine his business would have called him away just now, if he had not wished to avoid a certain gentleman, although it would appear that Wickham's absence was not after all so necessary, for that certain gentleman is not here either."

This part of his intelligence, though unheard by Luke, was caught by Edward, and he turned away with a degree of ill-humour, which he could not wholly surmount even when greeted with great cordiality by Mr Bingley, whose blindness to the situation provoked him.

But, despite the dashing of his hopes, Edward was not formed for ill-humour; and this was to be the last social occasion he would spend with his family for the foreseeable future, and so he contented himself with telling all his griefs to Charlotte Lucas, whom he had not seen to speak to for a week. In the course of their conversation, he made a voluntary transition to the oddities of their former tutor and now house-guest, and to remind her of his speech at Mrs Philips' party, which had caught her attention.

"What does Mr Collins mean by proposing himself to your family in this way?" asked Charlotte.

Edward recounted Mr Collins's reasons for returning to Longbourn, and was so much enjoying relaying the strangeness of Mr Collins' quest for a bride at Meryton, and his worship of his patroness, Lady Catherine De Bourgh, and his pride in his humble abode at Hunsford, that he failed to notice the expression on Charlotte's face.

When the dancing resumed, they stood up together, and Edward was pleased to see that Miss Bingley was standing up with John, with every appearance of complaisance and good-humour.

However, when those dances were over, and John led Mrs Hurst into the next two, Miss Bingley came towards them, and with an expression of civil disdain thus accosted Edward.

"So, Mr Edward Bennet, I hear you are quite delighted with George Wickham! Your brother has been talking to me about him, and asking me a thousand questions; and I find that the young man forgot to tell you, among his other communications, that he was the son of Old Wickham, the late Mr Darcy's steward. Let me recommend you, however, as my brother's friend, not to give implicit confidence to all his assertions; for as to Mr Darcy's using him ill, it is perfectly false; for, on the contrary, he has always been remarkably kind to him, though George Wickham has treated Mr Darcy in a most infamous manner. I do not know the particulars, but I know very well that Mr Darcy is not in the least to blame, that he cannot bear to hear George Wickham mentioned, and that though my brother thought he could not well avoid including him in his invitation to the officers, he was excessively glad to find that he had taken himself out of the way. However, Miss Darcy wished to go to London, and her brother is always happy to indulge her, so they were gone before today, and it matters not that Mr Wickham was invited. His coming into the country at all, is a most insolent thing indeed, and I wonder how he could presume to do it. I do not advise you to befriend George Wickham, indeed I do not, but really considering his descent, one could not expect him to be any better."

"I have heard you accuse him of nothing more than being the son of Mr Darcy's steward, and of that, I assure you, he informed me himself."

"I beg your pardon," replied Miss Bingley, turning away with a sneer, "But your family can hardly expect to gain any credence from such association, so my interference was kindly meant."

"Insolent girl!" said Edward to Charlotte, who had been standing by, silent and ignored by Miss Bingley during this exchange. "I see nothing in this paltry attack but her own wilful ignorance and the malice of Mr Darcy! Pray excuse me while I see if John has learned any thing useful from Mr Bingley."

Edward sought out John, who had undertaken to make inquiries of Mr Bingley regarding Mr Wickham. "I want to know, dear brother, what you have learnt about Mr Wickham from Mr Bingley? Any thing of any import, or any thing that Mr Wickham did not already tell me?"

"No," replied John, "I have nothing satisfactory to tell you. Mr Bingley does not know the whole of his history, and is quite ignorant of the circumstances which have principally offended Mr Darcy, but he will vouch for the good conduct, the probity and honour of his friend, and is perfectly convinced that Mr Wickham has deserved much less attention from Mr Darcy than he has received; and I am sorry to say that by his account Mr Wickham is by no means a respectable young man. I am afraid he has been very imprudent, and has deserved to lose Mr Darcy's regard."

"Mr Bingley does not know Mr Wickham himself?"

"No; he never saw him till the other morning at Meryton."

"This account then is what he has received from Mr Darcy. I am perfectly satisfied. But did he know any thing about the living Mr Wickham was promised?"

"He does not exactly recollect the circumstances, though he has heard from them from Mr Darcy more than once, but he believes that it was left to him   conditionally only."

"I have not a doubt of Mr Bingley's sincerity," said Edward warmly, "but you must excuse my not being convinced by assurances only. Mr Bingley's defence of his friend was a very able one, I dare say, but since he is unacquainted with several parts of the story, and has learnt the rest from that friend himself, I shall venture still to think of both gentlemen as I did before. But tell me if you have learnt any thing about why Mr Darcy took his sister away before tonight?"

"No, not at all. But there is a man arrived here today who knows the Darcy family as he is their cousin. A Colonel Fitzwilliam; Mr Bingley would introduce you; I am sure."

"But what is Mr Darcy's cousin doing here, at Netherfield?"

"I believe he is the Colonel of an Army regiment, and was passing by. His last intelligence was that Mr Darcy was at Netherfield, and so he called hoping to see him, but missed him and Miss Darcy by a day."

Edward asked Mr Bingley for an introduction to Colonel Fitzwilliam, which was most obligingly given. They took a turn about the room, talking of the current situation, and of the surprising absence of Mr and Miss Darcy.

"He likes to have his own way very well," said Colonel Fitzwilliam, "But so we all do. It is only that he has better means of having it than many others, because he is rich, and many others are poor. I speak feelingly. A younger son, as you know, must be inured to self-denial and dependence."

Although this was not to be Edward's experience, he assented civilly; and said, "I wonder that he does not marry, to secure a lasting convenience of having some body at his disposal. But, perhaps his sister does as well for the present, and, as she is under his sole care, he may do what he likes with her."

"No," said Colonel Fitzwilliam, "that is an advantage which he must divide with me. I am joined with him in the guardianship of Miss Darcy."

"Are you indeed? And, pray, what sort of guardians do you make? Does your charge give you much trouble? Young ladies of her age, are sometimes a little difficult to manage, although from my observation, Miss Darcy is a dutiful sister."

As Edward spoke, he observed Colonel Fitzwilliam looking at him earnestly, and the manner in which he   immediately asked why Mr Bennet should suppose Miss Darcy likely to give them any uneasiness, convinced Edward that he had somehow or other got pretty near the truth. But he directly replied,

"You need not be frightened. I never heard any harm of her; and I dare say she is one of the most tractable creatures in the world. She is a very great favourite of the Bingley family, and is often staying with them. I was just surprized that she should go away before this ball. I thought all young ladies loved to dance."

"I gather that Mr Darcy removed his sister from Netherfield due to the inconvenience of being in the same society as a particular young man to whom he has strong objections."

"And what were Miss Darcy's feelings upon this subject?"

"That I do not know."

They walked on a little, Edward's heart swelling with indignation.

"I am thinking of what you have told me," said he, "Your cousin's conduct does not suit my feelings. Why was he to be the judge of this man's suitability to be in the same society as his sister?"

"You are rather disposed to call his interference   officious?"

"I do not see what right Mr Darcy had to decide upon a matter which should have been of concern only to Miss Darcy, or why, upon his own judgement alone, this young man is to be considered unsuitable company. But," he continued, collecting himself, "as we know none of the particulars, it is not fair to condemn him. It is not to be supposed that there was much affection in the case."

"That is a not unnatural surmise," said Fitzwilliam, "But it is lessening the honour of Mr Darcy's action very sadly."

Edward turned the subject, and soon after made his bow, then recollecting that this was a ball, and that there were ladies present without partners; he turned his attention to the dancing. Mr Collins had, it appeared, made himself known to Charlotte Lucas, and they were sitting together, engaged in conversation.

When the ball came to an end, the Longbourn party were the last of the company to depart; and by a manoeuvre of Mrs Bennet had to wait for their carriages a quarter of an hour after every body else was gone, which gave them time to see how heartily they were wished away by some of the family. Mr and Mrs Hurst scarcely opened their mouths except to complain of fatigue; they were evidently impatient to have the house to themselves. repulsed every attempt of Mrs Bennet at conversation, and by so doing, threw a languor over the whole party, which was little relieved by the long speeches of Mr Collins, who was engaged in complimenting Mr Bingley and his sisters on the elegance of their entertainment, and the hospitality and politeness which had marked their behaviour to their guests. Mr Bingley said what was necessary in response to Mr Collins, but was scarcely attended to by that gentleman. Miss Bingley and John were standing together, a little detached from the rest, and talked only to each other. Edward preserved as steady as silence as the Hursts; and Mr Bennet, in equal silence, was enjoying the scene. Even Luke was much too fatigued to utter more than the occasional exclamation of, "Lord, how tired I am!" accompanied by a violent yawn.

When at last they rose to take their leave, Mrs Bennet was most pressingly civil in her hope of seeing the whole family soon at Longbourn; and the Darcys too, should they come back into the country; and assured them all how happy it would make every body, by eating a family dinner with them at any time, without the ceremony of a formal invitation. Bingley was all grateful pleasure, and he readily engaged for taking the earliest opportunity of waiting on her, after his return from London,

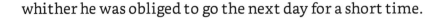

whither he was obliged to go the next day for a short time.

Chapter Seventeen

The next day opened a new scene at Longbourn. Mr Collins made his declaration in form. Having resolved to do without loss of time, as his leave of absence extended only to the following Saturday, and having no feelings of diffidence to make it distressing to himself even at the moment, he set about it in a very orderly manner, with all the observances which he supposed a regular part of the business.

Soon after breakfast, finding Mrs Bennet and one of the younger sons together, he begged that the Bennets would excuse him for the morning, as he had some important business to attend to.

"Oh, yes, certainly," Mrs Bennet answered, although she had not a notion of what business he could be attending to so far from home.

At the ball the previous evening, Charlotte Lucas had deliberately engaged Mr Collins in conversation, with the intention of securing his addresses. Such was her scheme; and appearances had been so favourable, that when they parted at the end of the ball, she would have felt almost sure of success if he had not been to leave Hertfordshire so very soon. But here, she did injustice to the fire and independence of his character, for it led him to excuse himself from Longbourn House that very morning, and hasten to Lucas Lodge to throw himself at her feet. He was anxious to avoid the Bennets' noticing the direction he was taking, from a conviction that they would conjecture his design, and he was not willing to have the attempt known till its success could be known likewise; for though feeling almost secure, and with reason, for Charlotte had been most encouraging, he did not wish to be thought of as a failure should he have been mistaken in her.

His reception however was of the most flattering kind. Miss Lucas perceived him from an upper window as he walked toward the house, and instantly set out to meet him accidentally in the lane. But little had she dared to hope that so much love and eloquence awaited her there.

"My dear Miss Lucas," cried he, "what happy chance brings you in my way this morning?"

Charlotte curtsied. "Good morning, sir. This is indeed a happy chance."

"Will you walk with me?"

Charlotte nodded, and shyly took his offered arm.

"I expect, my dear Miss Lucas," began Mr Collins, "that you can hardly doubt the purport of my seeking you out thus; however your natural delicacy may lead you to doubt, my attentions have been too marked to be mistaken. Almost as soon as I saw you, I singled you out as the companion of my future life. But before I am run away with my feelings on this subject, perhaps it will be advisable for me to state my reasons for marrying – and moreover for coming into Hertfordshire with the design of selecting a wife, as I certainly did."

Miss Lucas gave a civil assent, and waited for him to come to the point, so she could accept his hand, his heart, and his humble abode at Hunsford.

"My reasons for marrying are, first, that I think it a right thing for every clergyman in easy circumstances (like myself) to set the example of matrimony in his parish. Secondly, that I am convinced it will add very greatly to my happiness; and thirdly – which perhaps I ought to have mentioned earlier, that it is the particular advice and recommendation of the very noble lady whom I have the honour of calling patroness. Twice has she condescended to give me her opinion (unasked too!) as I believe I wrote thus to Mr Bennet, but you will not have seen my letter, so I do not hesitate to repeat my words to you. It was but the very Saturday night before I left Hunsford – between our pools at quadrille, while Mrs Jenkinson was arranging Miss De Bourgh's foot-stool, that she said, "Mr Collins, you must marry. A clergyman like you must marry. Chuse properly, chuse a gentlewoman for my sake; and for your own, let her be an active useful sort of person, not brought up high, but able to make a small income go a good way. This is my advice. Find such a woman as soon as you can, bring her to Hunsford, and I will visit her." Allow me, my dear Miss Lucas, to observe, that I do not reckon the notice and kindness of Lady Catherine de Bourgh as among the least of the advantages in my power to offer you. You will find her manners beyond any thing I can describe; and your gentleness and sense will, I am convinced, be acceptable to her. Thus much for my general intention in favour of matrimony; it remains to be told why my views were directed to Longbourn instead of my own neighbourhood. There are no suitable young women at Hunsford, or Lady Catherine would have drawn them to my attention, and as I have no family any where else, I thought of the lively society I recalled when I was last staying at Longbourn, and of the kind attentions of Mr and Mrs Bennet to my comfort and future."

He paused to peer anxiously at Charlotte to see if she would be put off by knowing he had been tutor to the Bennet sons, but Charlotte preserved a steady countenance, and begged him to continue.

"Nothing remains for me but to assure you of the violence of my affections for you. To fortune I am perfectly indifferent, and shall make no demand of that nature of your father, since I am well aware that it could not be complied with, and that you can have but little fortune to bring to the matrimonial home. On that head, therefore, I shall be uniformly silent; and you may assure yourself that no ungenerous reproach shall ever pass my lips when we are married."

"You are too good, sir," Charlotte said, "and I am honoured to accept your proposal, if you are certain that I shall be acceptable to Lady Catherine, and if my father agrees."

"I cannot imagine her ladyship would at all disapprove of you. And you may be certain that when I have the honour of seeing her again, I shall speak in the highest terms of your modesty, economy, and other amiable qualifications."

"Then, sir," said Charlotte, "nothing remains but for you to speak to my father. If you will walk into the house with me?"

Thus, in as short a time as Mr Collins's long speeches would allow, every thing was settled between them to the satisfaction of both; and as they entered the house, he earnestly entreated Charlotte to name the day that was to make him the happiest of men; and though such a solicitation must be waived for the present, the lady felt no inclination to trifle with his happiness. The stupidity with which he was favoured by nature, must guard his courtship from any charm that could make a woman wish for its continuance. Miss Lucas had accepted him solely from the pure and disinterested desire of an establishment of her own, and to avoid becoming an old maid at last, and cared not how soon that establishment were gained.

Sir William and Lady Lucas were speedily applied to for their consent; and it was bestowed with a most joyful alacrity. Mr

Collins's present circumstances made it a most eligible match for their daughter to whom they could give little fortune, and his prospects of future wealth were exceedingly fair. Lady Lucas may have harboured hopes of installing her eldest daughter at Longbourn in the future as the wife of the next Mr Bennet, but this was a most unlooked for windfall; it would be a matter of great relief to her to have a daughter settled so well at last. The whole family in short were properly overjoyed on the occasion. The younger girls formed hopes of coming out a year or two sooner than they might otherwise have done; and the boys were, like Charlotte herself, relieved from their apprehension of Charlotte's dying an old maid, and needing to be supported by them when they grew up.

Charlotte was tolerably composed. She had gained her point, and had time to consider of it. Her reflections were in general satisfactory. Mr Collins to be sure was neither sensible nor agreeable; his society was irksome, and his attachment to her must be imaginary. But still he would be her husband. Without thinking highly either of men or of matrimony, marriage had always been her object; it was the only honourable provision for well-educated young women of small fortune, and however uncertain of giving happiness, must be their pleasantest preservative from want. This preservative she had now obtained; and at the age of twenty-seven, without having ever been handsome, she felt all the good luck of it. The least agreeable circumstance in the business, was having to leave Meryton and all her friends, especially John and Edward Bennet, forever. They would wonder at her decision, and though her resolution was not to be shaken, her feelings would be hurt by their disapprobation. She resolved to give them the information herself, and therefore charged Mr Collins when he returned to Longbourn to dinner, to drop no hint of what had passed before any of the Bennet family. A promise of secrecy was of course very dutifully given, but it could not be kept without difficulty; for the curiosity excited by his long absence, burst forth in such very direct questions on his return, as required some ingenuity to evade, and he was at the same time exercising great self-denial, as he was longing to publish his prosperous love.

As he was to begin his journey back to Hunsford too early on the morrow to see any of the family, the ceremony of leave-taking was performed when everyone moved for the night; and Mrs Bennet with great politeness and cordiality said how happy they should be to see him at Longbourn again, whenever his other engagements might allow him to visit them.

"My dear Madam," he replied, "this invitation is particularly gratifying, because it is what I have been hoping to receive; and you may be very certain that I shall avail myself of it as soon as possible."

They were all astonished; and Mr Bennet, who could by no means wish for speedy a return, immediately said,

"But is there not danger of Lady Catherine's disapprobation here, my good sir? You had better neglect your friends than run the risk of offending your patroness."

"My dear Mr Bennet," replied Mr Collins,

"I am particularly obliged to you for this friendly caution, and you may depend upon my not taking so material a step without her ladyship's concurrence."

"You cannot be too much on your guard. Risk any thing other than her displeasure, and if you find it likely to be raised by your coming to us again, which I should think exceedingly probable, stay quietly at home, and be satisfied that we shall take no offence."

"Believe me, my dear sir, my gratitude is warmly excited by such affectionate attention; and depend upon it, you will speedily receive a letter of thanks for this, as well as for every other mark of your regard during my stay in Hertfordshire."

With proper civilities, all then withdrew; all of them equally surprised to find that he meditated a quick return. But then, as far as they knew, he had not succeeded in his stated aim in coming into the country; that of finding a bride.

But on the following morning, every thing became clear. Charlotte Lucas called soon after breakfast, and in a private conference with Edward and John, related the event of the day before.

The possibility of Mr Collins selecting Charlotte had once occurred to Edward within the last day or two; especially as she had spent so much time with him at the ball. But that Charlotte should encourage him herself, was so greatly astonishing, that Edward overcame the bounds of decorum, and couldn't help crying out,

"Engaged to Mr Collins! My dear Charlotte – impossible!"

John put his hand on Edward's arm, and begged Charlotte's pardon.

"We are delighted for you both," he said, but Charlotte replied to Edward's out-burst,

"Why should you find this impossible, Edward? Do you think Mr Collins so unlikely to procure my good opinion?"

With John's steadying influence beside him, Edward now recollected himself, and making a strong effort for it, was able to assure Charlotte with tolerable firmness that the prospect of this marriage was highly grateful to him, and that he wished her all imaginable happiness.

"I know what you are feeling," replied Charlotte, "It is all so very sudden; and I barely know Mr Collins, but when you have time to think it over, I hope you will see that I have done the right thing by this. I am not romantic you know. I never was. I ask only a comfortable home; and considering Mr Collins's character, connections, and situation in life, I am convinced that my chance of happiness with him is as fair, as most people can boast on entering the marriage state."

Edward quietly answered, "Undoubtedly," and left John to

make stronger expressions of happiness on both their accounts. Charlotte did not stay much longer, and Edward was left to reflect on what she had done. It was a long time before he became at all reconciled to the idea of so unsuitable a match.

Edward had always suspected that Charlotte's opinion of matrimony was an unusual one for a woman, but he would not have supposed it possible that when called into action, she would have sacrificed every better feeling to worldly advantage. Charlotte the wife of Mr Collins was a most humiliating picture for their childhood friend; and Edward had the distressing conviction that it was impossible for her to be tolerably happy in the lot she had chosen.

But he had no more time to repine, for the Fellowes's carriage was due to collect him; and his goodbyes had now to be made to his family. That they were markedly different to those of Mr Collins, may be imagined. But the distress of his father sincerely affected Edward, while the indifference of the younger two threw it in to even sharper contrast, and even his mother was not much upset, although she held a handkerchief to her eyes, and declared many times how her nerves were affected by his going away forever.

"Depend upon it, I will write to you very often," Edward assured his father, and John. "And the Gardiners are here at Christmas to cheer you up."

And he stept into the carriage and was gone.

Chapter Eighteen

The remaining Bennets returned into the house, Mr Bennet went in to his study, and John was wondering whether he was authorised to tell his mother and brothers about Charlotte and Mr Collins, when Sir William Lucas himself appeared, sent by his daughter to announce her engagement to the family. With many compliments to them, and much self-gratulation on the prospect of a great connection between his house and that of Lady Catherine de Bourgh, he unfolded the matter – to an audience not merely wondering, but incredulous; for Mrs Bennet, with more perseverance than politeness, protested he must be entirely mistaken, Mr Collins had but just quitted them and never dropt a word of this, and had not Charlotte been at Longbourn that very morning and not dropt a word; the sly thing!

Nothing less than the complaisance of a courtier could have borne without anger such treatment; but Sir William's good breeding carried him through it all; and though he begged leave to be positive as to the truth of his information, he listened to the impertinence with the most forbearing courtesy.

It was left to John to relieve Sir William from so unpleasant a situation, and he now put himself forward to confirm his account, by mentioning his prior knowledge of it from Charlotte herself; and endeavoured to put a stop to the exclamations of his mother and brothers, by heart-felt, earnest and gentle congratulations to Sir William. While the rest gaped in astonishment, John made a variety of remarks on the happiness that might be expected from such a match, the excellent character of Mr Collins, and the convenient distance of Hunsford from London.

Mrs Bennet was in fact too much overpowered to say a great deal while Sir William remained; but no sooner had he left them than her feelings found a rapid vent. In the first place, she persisted in disbelieving the whole of the matter; secondly, she was very sure that Mr Collins had been taken in, for he must not know that Sir William could do very little for Charlotte; thirdly she trusted that they would never be happy together; and fourthly, that the match might be broken off. She felt barbarously used by them all; to think that Mr Collins was staying at their house and making matches with so undeserving a young woman! Nothing could console and nothing appease her. A month passed away before she could speak to Sir William or Lady Lucas without being rude, and many months were gone before she could at all forgive their daughter. Her only consolation, indeed, was that John was safe from so designing a hussy.

Mr Bennet's emotions were much more tranquil on the occasion, and such as he did experience, he pronounced to be of a most agreeable sort; for it gratified him, he said, to discover that Charlotte Lucas, whom he had been used to think tolerably sensible, was as foolish as his wife, and more foolish than his younger sons!

John expressed the surprise he had not been able to express to Charlotte's face, in his first letter to Edward in his new home in Derbyshire. But went on to say less of astonishment than of his earnest desire for their happiness, and hoped that, by now, Edward would also be able to concede that it was not improbable.

Charles and Luke were entirely indifferent to Charlotte's triumph, for Mr Collins was only a clergyman; and their marriage affected them in no other way than as a piece of news that they had before their aunt Philips, to spread at Meryton.

Lady Lucas could not be insensible of triumph on being able to retort upon Mrs Bennet the comfort of having a child well married; and she called at Longbourn rather oftener than usual to say how happy she was, though Mrs Bennet's sour looks and ill-natured remarks might have been enough to drive happiness away.

With Edward gone, and Mr Collins gone, the remaining Bennets' attention turned back to the Bingleys. They were also gone; and no body seemed to know when they would return.

The promised letter from Mr Collins arrived on Tuesday, addressed to Mr Bennet, and written with all the solemnity of gratitude which a twelvemonth's abode in the family might have prompted. After discharging his conscience on that head, he proceeded to inform them, with many rapturous expressions, of his happiness in having obtained the affection of their amiable neighbour, Miss Lucas, and then explained that it was merely with the view of enjoying her society that he had been so ready to close with their kind wish of seeing him again at Longbourn, whither he hoped to be able to return on Monday fortnight; for Lady Catherine, he added, so heartily approved his marriage, that she wished it to take place as soon as possible, which he trusted would be an unanswerable argument with his amiable Charlotte to name an early day for making him the happiest of men.

Mrs Bennet was not mollified by these fine phrases, and nor could she find any comfort in the mention of Lady Catherine. On the contrary she could not understand why Mr Collins should not go to Lucas Lodge instead of Longbourn, and she was as much disposed to complain of his returning so soon, as her husband. It was very strange that he should come to Longbourn instead of to Lucas Lodge; it was also very inconvenient and exceedingly troublesome. She hated having visitors in the house, while her health was so indifferent, and lovers were of all people the most disagreeable. Such were the gentle murmurs of Mrs Bennet, and they gave way only to the greater distress of Mr Bingley's continued absence, for she had it from Mrs Long, that the house had been shut up, and there were no plans for the family to return this side of Christmas. Here was a sad end to all her hopes for John marrying Miss Bingley, or for Mr Bingley's influence in getting good places for her sons; although she appeared to have forgot that three out of the five were settled already.

Mr Collins returned most punctually on the Monday fortnight, but his reception at Longbourn was not quite so gracious as it had been on his first introduction.

He was too happy, however, to need much attention; and luckily for the Bennets, the business of love-making relieved them from a great deal of his company. The chief of every day was spent by his at Lucas Lodge, and he sometimes returned to Longbourn only in time to make an apology for his absence before the family went to bed.

After a week spent in professions of love and schemes of felicity, Mr Collins was called from his amiable Charlotte by the arrival of Saturday. The pain of separation, however, might be alleviated on his side, by preparations for the reception of his bride, as he had reason to hope, that shortly after his next return into Hertfordshire, the day would be fixed that was to make him the happiest of men. He took leave of the Bennet family with as much solemnity as before; wished them all health and happiness again, and promised Mr Bennet another letter of thanks.

John kept Edward abreast of all developments at Longbourn with regard to Mr Collins, Charlotte, and the Bingleys. Edward had heard nothing of the Darcys since his arrival into Derbyshire, even though the Fellowes's new estate bordered on the

Pemberley estate. It was, Edward wrote to John, strange to be in so small a family group, after so many years with all his brothers growing up; but there were compensations, as he felt sure John could imagine and sympathise with.

"There is both comfort and elegance in my new family party; and all it wants to be perfect is your company. I hope you will come into the country to visit in the coming year; Mr and Mrs Fellowes will welcome you warmly, I am convinced. But tell me more of the Bingleys' absence from Netherfield; will Mr Morris let it again after Christmas, think you? And what of Charlotte's marriage to Mr Collins? It is unaccountable! In every view it is unaccountable!"

John replied, thus,

"My dear Edward, do not give way to feelings such as these; they will ruin your happiness in your new situation, with your new family. Charlotte has long been our friend, and we should always wish the best for our friends. You do not make allowances for difference of situation and temper. Consider Mr Collins's respectability, and Charlotte's prudent, steady character. Remember that she is one of a large family; that as to fortune, it is a most eligible match; and be ready to believe, for every body's sake, that she may feel something like regard for him. As for the Bingleys; I hardly know what to think. It would seem that their removing from Netherfield was to allow stronger ties between their two families, without the dilution of additional company. But it is nearly Christmas time and we are to welcome my uncle and aunt Gardiner and their children, and there will be many parties and much happiness to relate in my next letter."

Edward could not see Charlotte's marriage in the same forgiving light as his brother. As far as he was concerned, Mr Collins was a pompous, conceited, narrow-minded, silly man; and that the woman who married him, could not have a proper way of thinking. There was no profit in continuing to disapprove at such a distance, however, and so he turned his attention to his first Christmas with his new family. There was much to console him in the gift of his own horse to ride about the estate, and in beginning to work with Mr Fellowes on the management of this estate, and getting to know the neighbourhood; that his former home soon seemed another life time ago.

Chapter Nineteen

After Mr Collins's final departure, Mrs Bennet had the pleasure of receiving her brother and his wife, who came as usual to spend the Christmas at Longbourn. Mr Gardiner was a sensible, gentlemanlike man, greatly superior to his sister as well by nature as education. The Netherfield ladies would have had difficulty in believing that a man who lived by trade, and within sight of his own warehouses, could have been so well bred and agreeable. Mrs Gardiner, who was several years younger than Mrs Bennet and Mrs Philips, was an amiable, intelligent, elegant woman, and a great favourite of all her Longbourn nephews. For her part, she had a particular regard for the eldest two, and was most sorry to have missed seeing Edward this year; he and John had an open invitation to visit her in town.

The first part of Mrs Gardiner's business on her arrival, was to distribute her presents and describe the newest fashions to her sisters. When this was over, she had a less active part to play. It became her turn to listen, and Mrs Bennet had many grievances to relate, and much to complain of. They had all be very ill-used since she last saw her sister. "However," she ended with, "your coming just at this time is the greatest of comforts, and I am very glad to hear what you tell us, of long sleeves."

Mrs Gardiner, to whom the chief of this news had been already imparted in the course of her correspondence with John and Edward, made her sister a slight answer, and turned the conversation.

When alone briefly with John later, Mrs Gardiner asked if he would be prevailed upon to go back with them to London after Christmas. A change of scene is always of service, and a little relief from home, may be as useful as any thing. John was exceedingly pleased with this proposal, and made a ready acquiescence.

"It is not very possible," added Mrs Gardiner, "that we may see something of the Bingleys or Darcys, for we live in so different a part of town, all our connections are so different, and as you well know, we go out so little, that it is not very likely you should meet them at all, unless you seek them out at their town houses."

When John relayed this invitation to Edward, the response was,

"Mr Darcy may well have heard of such a place as Gracechurch Street, but he would hardly think a month's ablution enough to cleanse him from its impurities, were he once to enter it; and depend upon it, Mr Bingley never stirs without him."

Which showed that Edward, at least, had not forgiven Mr Darcy for either his ill-treatment of Wickham, nor for whisking Miss Darcy away in the belief that a Mr Edward Bennet was an unsuitable acquaintance for her.

The Gardiners staid a week at Longbourn; and what with the Philipses, the Lucases, and the officers, there was not a day without its engagement. Mrs Bennet had so carefully provided for the entertainment of her brother and sister, that they did not once sit down to a family dinner. When the engagement was at home, some of the officers were always made part of it, of which officers Mr Wickham was sure to be one, and he had one means of affording pleasure to Mrs Gardiner, unconnected with his general powers. About ten or a dozen years ago, before her marriage, she had spent a considerable time in that very part of Derbyshire, to which he belonged. They had, therefore, many acquaintance in common; and, though Wickham had been little there since the death of Darcy's father, five years before, it was yet in his power to give her fresher intelligence of her former friends, than she had been in the way of procuring.

Mrs Gardiner had seen Pemberley, and known the late Mr Darcy by character perfectly well. Here consequently was an inexhaustible subject of discourse. In comparing her recollection of Pemberley, with the minute description which Wickham could give, and in bestowing her tribute of praise on the character of its late possessor, she was delighting both him and herself. On being made acquainted with the present Mr Darcy's treatment of him, she tried to remember something of that gentleman's reputed disposition when quite a lad, which might agree with it, and was confident at last, that she recollected having heard Mr Fitzwilliam Darcy formerly spoken of as a very proud, ill-natured boy.

Mr Collins returned into Hertfordshire soon after it had been quitted by the Gardiners and John; but as he took up his abode with the Lucases, his arrival was no great inconvenience to Mrs Bennet. His marriage was now fast approaching, and she was at length so far resigned as to think it inevitable, and even repeatedly to say in an ill-natured tone that she "wished they might be happy." Thursday was to be the wedding day, and on Wednesday Miss Lucas paid her farewell visit; and when she rose to take leave, John, ashamed of his mother's ungracious and reluctant good wishes, and sincerely affected himself by the loss of his childhood friend, escorted her to the door. As they went down stairs together, Charlotte said,

"I hope you and Edward will remember me kindly, John. We have been friends all our lives."

"That we certainly shall."

"My father and Maria come to me in March," added Charlotte, "so I will hear news of you all, unless you or Edward will write to me?"

John undertook to keep her informed of what was passing in Meryton and the Bennet family news. The wedding took place; the bride and bridegroom set off for Kent from the church door, and every body had as much to say or to hear on the subject as usual. John made sure to send Edward a full account and to pass on Charlotte's request for correspondence. This both Bennets honoured; but there was a reservation in the correspondence that could only signify that the comfort of intimacy was at an end with Charlotte's marriage.

Charlotte's own first letters were received with a good deal of eagerness; there could not but be curiosity to know how she would speak of her new home, how she would like Lady Catherine, and how happy she would dare pronounce herself to be; though, when the letters were read, Edward and John agreed that she had expressed herself on every point exactly as they might have foreseen. Charlotte wrote cheerfully, seemed surrounded with comforts, and mentioned nothing which she could not praise. The house, furniture, neighbourhood, and roads, were all to her taste, and Lady Catherine's behaviour was most friendly and obliging. It was Mr Collins's picture of Hunsford and Rosings rationally softened; and Edward perceived that the exact truth was likely to remain hid from him.

John had also written a few lines to announce his safe arrival in London; and when he wrote again, Edward hoped it would be in his power to say something of the Bingleys, or Darcys. His impatience for a second letter was as well rewarded as impatience generally is. John had been a week in town without either seeing or hearing from Mr Bingley. He accounted for it, however, by supposing that his last letter from Longbourn, had by some accident been lost.

"My aunt," he continued," he continued, "is going tomorrow into that part of the town, and I shall take the opportunity of calling in to Grosvenor Street."

He wrote again when the visit was paid, and he had seen both Mr and Miss Bingley. "I did not think them in spirits," were his words, "but they were glad to see me and reproached me for giving no notice of my coming to London. I was right, therefore; my last letter had never reached them. I enquired after the Darcys of course; they were well, but much engaged with friends and acquaintances of their own, and they scarcely ever saw them. I found, however, that they were expected to dinner. I wish I could have seen them, so I could give you an account of how they looked. My visit was not long, as Caroline and Mrs Hurst were going out, and Mr Bingley had to attend them. I dare say I shall soon see them here."

Edward shook his head over this letter. It convinced him that the Bingleys were not keen to continue the acquaintance, and that Mr Darcy was still shielding his sister from all potentially dangerous young men.

Four weeks passed away and the Bingleys did not return John's call. After waiting at home every morning for a fortnight, and inventing every evening a fresh excuse, Miss Bingley did at last appear, but the shortness of her stay, and yet more, the alteration of her manners, would allow him to deceive himself no longer. The letter which he wrote on this occasion to Edward, will prove what he felt.

"My dear Edward will, I am sure, be incapable of triumphing in his better judgement, at my expence, when I confess myself to have been entirely deceived in Miss Bingley's regard for me. But, though the event has proved you right, do not think me obstinate if I still assert, that, considering what her behaviour was at Netherfield, my confidence was as natural as your suspicion. I do not at all comprehend her reasons for appearing to wish for my addresses, but if the same circumstances were to happen again, I am sure I should be deceived again; I shall struggle to find another I can prefer to her. Miss Bingley did not return my visit until yesterday, but she came alone, as I requested in a note. However, it was evident that she came only because of the note, and that she had no pleasure in the visit; she made a slight, formal apology for not calling before, said not a word of wishing to see me again, and was in every aspect so altered a creature, that when she went away, I realised I could not expect to continue the acquaintance any longer. She made slighting reference to a friend of her's who had contracted a mesalliance, in her phrase, by marrying a gentleman who lived on a very small estate, and whose income was derived from farming that estate. She said that her friend had thus cut herself off from all good society, and that Caroline could no longer visit her or have any thing to do with her. Her meaning could not have been clearer; I am beneath her notice, and so I did not make her my offer. She was very wrong in singling me out as she did; I can safely say, that every advance to intimacy began on her side, and I followed her lead. I need not explain myself further to you; I am sure. She also mentioned how much they are hoping that Mr Bingley will make an offer to Miss Darcy soon, and that Mr Bingley does not intend to return to Netherfield again; that he will give up the house, but not with any certainty. We had better not mention it. I am extremely glad to hear from Charlotte Collins with such very good accounts of her new life; it is very pleasing indeed that she is so well settled and happy."

This letter gave Edward some pain; but his spirits returned as he considered that John would no longer be duped by Miss Bingley. Her character sunk on every review of it; and as a punishment for her, Edward hoped she might soon marry Mr Darcy, and make his life miserable instead of John's.

An unexpected letter from Charles followed with news of Mr Wickham. His attentions had been captured by a young woman but lately arrived in Meryton, and whose most remarkable charm was as the recipient of the sudden acquisition of ten thousand pounds. Wickham had paid her not the smallest attention until her grandfather's death made her mistress of his fortune, and he was not now interested in his acquaintance with Luke and Charles; all was Miss King with him, and he attended no parties or dinners if Miss King were not invited. Edward could not quarrel with Mr Wickham's wish for independence; nothing on the contrary, could be more natural than he should attempt to bring himself to the attention of a young woman with a fortune. Charles had nothing good to say about Miss King; but knowing nothing of her himself, Edward preferred to suppose that she was a very good sort of girl, and wondered if some of John's charity was at last rubbing off on him. Charles and Luke would learn in time that handsome young men must have something to live on as well as the plain.

Chapter Twenty

Mrs Gardiner, fond as she was of her nephew, could not help noticing the lowness of his spirits following Miss Bingley's visit. It grieved more than astonished her to see that though John always struggled to support his spirits so as not to give her pain, there were yet periods of dejection, despite the presence of a troop of little boys and girls, whose joy in their cousin's visit was very great indeed, and despite all the bustle of a busy household, shopping, and evenings at one of the theatres. But there was the prospect of a northern tour to raise John's spirits; his uncle and aunt intended to go into Derbyshire in the summer, to visit the places Mrs Gardiner had known before her marriage, and to pay their respects to Mr and Mrs Fellowes.

No scheme could have been more agreeable to John, and his acceptance of the invitation was most ready and grateful. He was to return home in the mean time; and so it was the second week in May, when he left Gracechurch-street, for the town of -- in Hertfordshire; where Mr Bennet's carriage was to meet him at an appointed inn. John soon perceived, in token of the coachman's punctuality, both Charles and Luke looking out of a dining room window up stairs. They had been above an hour in the place, happily employed in walking up and down the street, and ordering a dressed salad and cucumber.

After welcoming John, they triumphantly displayed a table set out with such cold meat as an inn larder usually affords, exclaiming, "Is not this nice? Is not this an agreeable surprise?"

"And we mean to treat you," added Luke, "but you must lend us the money, for we have none."

As soon as all had ate, and John had paid, the carriage was ordered. As the it moved through the town, Charles and Luke hung out of the windows, calling out to the young woman passing, and abusing them to each other.

"Look at that quiz of a bonnet!"

"Indeed! it is very ugly!"

"There are two or three much uglier in that shop we just passed."

When they were finally out of the town, Luke and Charles settled back to give John the latest news from their aunt in Meryton.

"Just before we left, my aunt told us that the –shire are to leave Meryton, and they are going in a fortnight."

"Are they indeed?" replied John.

"They are going to be encamped near Brighton; and I do so want papa to take us all there for the summer! It would be such a scheme and a joke, and I dare say would hardly cost any thing at all. Mamma would like to go too of all things! Only think what a miserable summer else we shall have!"

"Now I have some news for you," Charles put in, "what do you think? It is excellent news, capital news, and about a certain person that we all like."

"Who can it be?" John asked, his mind running over all the people they all liked.

"It is about Mr Wickham. There is no danger of his marrying Mary King. There's for you! She is gone down to her uncle at Liverpool; gone to stay. Wickham is safe, and can come to our aunt's parties again, without her being there to distract him."

"I hope there is no strong attachment on either side," said John.

"I am sure there is not on his," Luke cried, "I will answer for it he never cared three straws about her. Who could about such a nasty little freckled thing?"

With such news and histories of their parties and good jokes, did Luke, assisted by Charles's hints and additions, endeavour to amuse his eldest brother all the way to Longbourn. John's reception at home was most kind. Mrs Bennet was glad to have him back safe from London, and more than once during dinner did Mr Bennet say voluntarily, "I am glad you are come back, John."

Their party in the dining room was large, for almost all the Lucases came, and John found himself sitting next to Maria Lucas, who had more to tell about her sister's welfare and poultry. Luke and Charles were retailing all the pleasures of the morning to any body who would hear, in a voice rather louder than any other person's.

"Oh! Mark," said he, "I wish you had gone with us, for we had such fun! As we went along, Charles and me drew up all the blinds, and pretended there was nobody in the coach; and I should have gone so all the way, if Charlie had not been sick; and when we got to the George, I do think we behaved handsomely, for we treated John with the nicest cold luncheon in the world, and if you would have gone, we would have treated you too. And then when we came away it was such fun! I thought we never should have got into the coach. I was ready to die of laughter at some of the people we saw on the way home. And then we were so merry, we talked and laughed so loud, that any body might have heard us ten miles off!"

To this Mark gravely replied, "You forget, my dear brother, that I was at work today, but far be it from me to depreciate such pleasures as you describe. They would doubtless be congenial to many people's minds. But I confess they would have no charms for me. I should infinitely prefer a book."

But of this answer Luke heard not a word. He seldom listened to any body for more than half a minute, and never attended to

Mark at all.

In the afternoon Luke was urgent for the family to walk into Meryton and see how every body went on; but John steadily opposed the scheme. The regiment was to decamp, and it seemed pointless to chase after the officers now; they would soon be gone. John had not been many hours at home, before he found that the Brighton scheme, of which Luke had given him a hint at the inn, was under frequent discussion between his parents. John could see directly that his father had not the smallest intention of yielding; but his answers were at the same time so vague and equivocal, that his mother, though often disheartened, had never yet despaired of succeeding at last.

John acquainted his parents with the scheme to go into Derbyshire with Mr and Mrs Gardiner; to see the sights, and to pay their respects to Mr and Mrs Fellowes, come the summer; and Mr Bennet handed him an envelope from Edward himself, which had arrived under cover of a letter to himself. John took himself off in to the arbour to read it.

"My dear brother, I must relate something to you which is both shocking and surprizing; I feel no doubt of your secrecy, though I have not been authorised to share this information with you. But be not alarmed; I am well, as are Mr and Mrs Fellowes, and I am happy beyond words that you will be coming this summer with my uncle and aunt, into Derbyshire.

As you know, Mr Fellowes has bought for me a fine horse, and I have been riding around his estate, and becoming acquainted with the people in our neighbourhood. On one of my rides a few weeks ago, I encountered, to my complete surprise, Miss Darcy, out riding with a companion. She was pleased to see me, and we renewed the conversations that gave us both such pleasure when she was staying at Netherfield. Subsequent to that, we met frequently, out riding, or walking, always with her companion, a Mrs Annesley as chaperone. I ventured to open my heart to Miss Darcy, and in return, she related to me the following history, which she hoped would not give me a disgust of her, and which explained why Mr Darcy removed her from Nether-field before the ball.

You will recall what Colonel Fitzwilliam told me? That Mr Darcy had removed his sister due to a very unsuitable young man in the country? I thought that I was that unsuitable young man, but it was not me, but instead our old friend Mr Wickham! There! What say you to that? I begged Miss Darcy to explain more and assured her that what ever she was to tell me would not diminish my sincere regard for her, and she was emboldened to continue.

Mr Wickham was indeed the favourite of Miss Darcy's father, and he was promised a valuable living on the Pemberley estate when Mr Darcy died, and when the living became vacant. There was also a legacy of one thousand pounds. Mr Wickham died very soon after Mr Darcy, and our Mr Wickham wrote to Mr Darcy to inform him that, having finally resolved against taking orders, he hoped for some more immediate pecuniary advantage, as he could not live upon the interest of one thousand pounds. So Mr Darcy gave him another three thousand pounds, and dissolved all connection between them. Miss Darcy does not know what her brother knew to Mr Wickham's discredit, but she is sure it is that he was vicious and not at all respectable.

On the decease of the incumbent of the living which had been designated for Mr Wickham, he applied again by letter to Mr Darcy for the presentation, and was refused. He intruded upon the Darcy family notice, and it was here that Miss Darcy became distressed, for this matter touched her very nearly. About a year ago, she was taken from school, and an establishment was formed for her in London; and last summer she went with the lady who presided over it (not Mrs Annesley, but a Mrs Younge, in whose character Mr Darcy had been most unhappily deceived), to Ramsgate; and thither also went Mr Wickham, undoubtedly by design; for there proved to have been a prior acquaintance between him and Mrs Younge. By her connivance and aid, he so far recommended himself to Miss Darcy, whose affectionate heart retained a strong impression of his kindness to her as a child – you see how cleverly Mr Wickham blended fact with fiction when he told me his sad story! – that she was persuaded to believe herself in love, and to consent to an elopement.

She was then but fifteen, and doubtless Mr Wickham's first object was her fortune, which is thirty thousand pounds; but Miss Darcy also supposes that Mr Wickham was intending to revenge himself on her brother for refusing him the living he had been promised, and had given up voluntarily. She was unable to support the idea of grieving and offending her brother, whom she looks up to almost as a father, and so she acknowledged the whole to Mr Darcy. He acted immediately to protect and remove his sister from Ramsgate, Mr Wickham and Mrs Younge. When Mr Darcy saw Mr Wickham with us in the street at Meryton, he was horrified at the thought that Mr Wickham might try again, and so he and Miss Darcy left before the ball. Miss Darcy is now settled back at Pemberley, with Mrs Annesley, a most genteel, agreeable-looking woman, and completely trust-worthy, as her companion.

This, my dear brother, is the true story behind Mr Wickham's words, and Miss Darcy has authorised me to seek out the testimony of Colonel Fitzwilliam, who, sharing her guardianship with her brother, has been unavoidably acquainted with every particular, should I doubt her word. But I should not dream of doubting her, nor of blaming her; we both know how persuasive Mr Wickham could be. It is a great relief that the –shire is leaving Meryton, and all contact with Mr Wickham will soon be at an end.

What I wanted to ask you was; whether we ought, or ought not to make our acquaintance in general understand Wickham's character?"

When John had read thus far, he had to put the letter down; what a stroke this was for poor John! Who would willingly have gone through the world without believing that such wicked things could happen, nor that an individual he had befriended was capable of acting in such a wicked way.

His reply when it came to Edward, ran thus:

"I do not know when I have been more shocked. Wickham so very bad! It is almost past belief. And poor Mr and Miss Darcy! Dear Edward, only consider what they have both suffered. How brave of Miss Darcy to relate such a thing of herself; she must hold you in high regard to trust you thus. And to think there is such an expression of goodness in Wickham's countenance! Such an openness and gentleness in his manner. In answer to your question, surely there can be no occasion for exposing him so dreadfully. What is your own opinion?"

To which Edward replied:

"I do not think we ought to attempt to expose Mr Wickham. Miss Darcy has not authorised me to make her story public; on the contrary, with regard to her credit in society, this must be kept strictly to ourselves. And if we do endeavour to undeceive people as to the rest of his conduct, who will believe us? There is a general prejudice against Mr Darcy, that it would be the death of half the good people in Meryton, to attempt to place him in an amiable light. I do not believe you to be equal to it. Wickham will soon be gone; and therefore it will not signify to any body there, what he really is. Some time hence it will be found out, and then we may laugh at their stupidity for not knowing it before. At present, I counsel you to say nothing about it."

John agreed that Edward was quite right; to have his errors made public might ruin Wickham for ever; perhaps he was even now sorry for what he had done, and anxious to re-establish a character; it would not do to make him desperate, or cause him to be cast out of the Militia, now that he had a respectable occupation.

Chapter Twenty-one

In this way the two weeks between John returning from London and the regiment's leaving Meryton was gone, and all the young ladies in the neighbourhood were drooping apace. The dejection was almost universal. John was pleased to see that Maria Lucas alone appeared unaffected, and was cheerfully pursuing her usual course of employments, including paying them visits to give them the latest news from her sister. She was reproached for this insensitivity by Luke and Charles, whose own misery was extreme, and who could not comprehend such hard-heartedness in a young woman.

"Good Heaven! What is to become of us! What are we to do!" would they often exclaim, in the bitterness of woe. "How can you be smiling so, Maria?"

Their affectionate mother shared all their grief; she remembered what she herself had endured on a similar occasion, five and twenty years ago.

"I am sure," said she, "I cried for two days together when Colonel Millar's regiment went away. I thought I should have broke my heart."

"If one could but go to Brighton!" observed Charles.

"Oh, yes! If one could but go to Brighton! But papa is so disagreeable."

"A little sea-bathing would set me up for ever."

"And my aunt Philips is sure it would do me a good deal of good," added Charles.

Such were the lamentations resounding perpetually through Longbourn-house, in the face of Mr Bennet's implacability. But the gloom of Luke's prospect was shortly cleared away; for he received an invitation from Mrs Forster, to accompany the regiment to Brighton, to see what soldiering was really like; as Luke had told Colonel Forster he was wishing to enlist himself in the Militia.

The rapture of Luke on this occasion, his gratitude to Mrs Forster, the delight of Mrs Bennet, and the mortification of Charles, are scarcely to be described. Wholly inattentive to any body else's feelings, Luke flew about the house in restless exstacy, calling for every one's congratulations, and laughing and talking with more violence than ever; whilst the luckless Charles continued repining his fate in terms as unreasonable as his accent was peevish.

"I cannot see why Mrs Forster should not ask me as well as Luke," said he, "though I do not remind her of her brother, to be sure, I have just as much right to be asked as Luke, and more too, for I am two years older."

In vain did John attempt to make Charles see reason, or at least make him resigned. John himself was worried about this latest adventure of Luke, and wrote to Edward expressing his concern about the little advantage Luke could derive from the friendship of such a woman as Mrs Forster, even though he had hopes that this friendship would lead Colonel Forster to assist Luke to a lucrative commission. But, as Mr Bennet was not inclined to prevent Luke going, there was nothing that either John, nor Edward, could do to prevent it.

"My father says that Colonel Forster is a sensible man," John wrote to Edward in conclusion, "and will keep Luke out of any real mischief. At Brighton he will soon discover that soldiering is not as glamorous as he thinks, and he will return to us cured of red-coat fever."

With this, both John and Edward had to be content; they had performed their duty, and to fret over unavoidable evils, or augment them by anxiety, was no part of their disposition. Had Luke and his mother known the substance of the letters and conferences that had been flying back and forth over the two weeks, their indignation would hardly have found expression in their united volubility. Had Luke known that his eldest brothers had sought to tear him away from the prospects and realities that he imagined encampment life to be, what would have been his sensations? They would have been understood only by his mother, who might have felt nearly the same. Luke's going to Brighton was all that consoled her for the melancholy conviction of her husband's never intending to go there himself. But they were entirely ignorant of what had passed; and their raptures continued with little intermission to the very day of Luke's leaving home.

The Bennets were now to see Mr Wickham for the last time. Having been frequently in company with him since returning from London, John was able to detect in the very gentleness he had first noticed, an affectation and sameness to disgust and weary. In his present behaviour to the young ladies present, John had a fresh source of displeasure; knowing his actions with regard to Miss Darcy threw the question of Miss King in to his mind – had Mr Wickham put Miss King in danger? Was that why she was removed by her uncle to Liverpool?

These meditations were interrupted by Mr Wickham coming to say his good byes to John, and to pass on his best wishes to Edward. Knowing that John had seen something of the Bing-

ley family in London, Mr Wickham enquired whether Mr Darcy
were still of their party.

"I did not see him in London," John replied.

"Perhaps he is at Rosings, forwarding his match with Miss De
Bourgh," Wickham suggested.

"I cannot tell you."

The rest of the evening passed with the appearance, on his side,
of usual cheerfulness, but with no further attempts to speak
with John, or allude to his past grievances against Mr Darcy, and
they parted at last with mutual civility, and possibly a mutual
desire of never meeting again.

John could see now the impropriety of Wickham's behaviour
amongst strangers, and the inconsistency of his professions
with his conduct; which did not seem to have struck every body
else with equal force.

He wrote about this final meeting to Edward, ending thus;

'I remember you saying that he boasted of having no fear of
meeting Mr Darcy - that Mr Darcy might leave the country, but
that he should stand his ground; yet he avoided the Netherfield
ball the very next week. How did I not notice this? And now
that the militia is to be gone, I notice that every body knows
Wickham's sad history with Mr Darcy, although he told you that
respect for the father would always prevent him exposing the
son. It appears he has no reserves, no scruples in sinking Mr
Darcy's character once the Netherfield family quitted the country; and Wickham's story is everwhere discussed.'

When the party broke up, Luke returned with Colonel and Mrs
Forster to Meryton, from whence they were to set out early the
next morning. The separation between Luke and his family was
rather noisy than pathetic. Charles was the only one to shed
tears; but these were tears of frustration and envy. Mrs Bennet
was diffuse in her good wishes for the felicity and future of her
favourite son, and impressive in her injunctions that he would

not miss the opportunity of enjoying himself as much as possible; advice, which there was every reason to believe would be attended to; and in the clamorous happiness of Luke himself in bidding farewell, the more gentle adieus of Mark and John were uttered without being heard.

Chapter Twenty-two

Had Edward's opinion been all drawn from his own family, he could not have formed a very pleasing picture of conjugal felicity or domestic comfort. Even had he done so, it would not have prevented him paying his addresses to Miss Darcy, although he did not intend to make her an offer while her brother was still absent – he was expected home any day. They continued meeting on their rides around their estates, and every meeting deepened their mutual understanding, respect and affection.

Reflecting on his own parents now that he was no longer in the bosom of the family; Edward could see that his father had been captivated by youth and beauty, and that appearance of good humour, which youth and beauty generally give. He had married a woman whose weak understanding and illiberal mind, had very early in their marriage put an end to all real affection for her. This was clear to Edward now, and he both grieved for it, and determined that his own marriage would be completely the opposite. Miss Darcy was of like mind with Edward and was well-read, cultured and accomplished, even by the stringent standards set by Miss Bingley and Mr Darcy. Edward had not the smallest fear that their marriage would be one to shew the world what true conjugal felicity was like, and he was grateful to be marrying for love, and having a help-meet, and partner for life.

Mr Bennet was not, Edward was thankful, of a disposition to seek comfort for the disappointment which his own imprudence had brought on, in any of those pleasures which too often console the unfortunate for their folly or their vice. He was fond of the country, and of books; and from these tastes had arisen his principal enjoyments. To his wife he was very little otherwise indebted, than as her ignorance and folly had contributed to his amusement. This is not the sort of happiness that Edward sought with Miss Darcy, and nor is it the sort of happiness which a man would in general wish to owe to his wife; but where other powers of entertainment are wanting, the true philosopher will derive benefit from such as are given.

Edward could not now be blind to the impropriety of his father's behaviour as a husband, especially now that he had the examples of Mr Gardiner and Mr Fellowes before him. He now saw this with pain; but could respect his father's abilities, and was grateful for the affectionate attention he had always received, and which was selfless enough to allow Edward to be adopted by Mr and Mrs Fellowes. Edward endeavoured to forget what he could not overlook, and to banish from his thoughts that continual breach of conjugal obligation and decorum which, in exposing his wife to the contempt of her own children, was so highly reprehensible.

But he had never felt so strongly as now, the disadvantages which must attend the children of so unsuitable a marriage, nor ever been so fully aware of the evils arising from so ill-judged a direction of talents; talents which rightly used, might at least have assisted in the proper education of his sons in order to facilitate their placement in a respectable line of work, even if incapable of enlarging the mind of his wife. These were mistakes Edward was determined not make for himself within his own marriage.

As for John, still at home with Mr and Mrs Bennet; he was less inclined to analyse, nor be so dissatisfied with his home life. Wickham was gone, but there was little actual satisfaction to be had from the loss of the regiment. Their parties abroad were less varied than before; and at home was Mrs Bennet and Charles, whose constant repinings at the dullness of every thing around them, threw a real gloom over their domestic circle; and though Charles might in time regain his natural degree of sense, since the disturbers of his brain were removed, his younger brother was likely to be hardened in all his folly and assurance, by a situation of such double danger as a watering place and a camp. Upon the whole, as John wrote to Edward, what has been sometimes found before, that an event to which one looked forward to with impatient desire, did not in taking place, bring all the satisfaction one had assumed would follow. There were compensations in the company of Maria Lucas, who called in very often, and his tour into the north country was now the object of his happiest thoughts; it was his best consolation for all the uncomfortable hours, which the discontentedness of his mother and brother made inevitable; and there was the visit to Edward to look forward to as well.

When Luke went away, he promised to write very often and very minutely to his mother and brother; but his letters were always long expected and always very short. Those to his mother contained little else than they were just returned from here, or about to visit there, and such and such officers had given a party, but he was obliged to leave off now in a violent hurry, as Mrs Forster needed him to attend her, and they were going to the camp – and from his correspondence with Charles, there was still less to be learnt – for these letters, though rather longer, were much too full of lines under the words to be made public. There was never a letter for Mark, nor for John, and Luke appeared to have forgotten he had another brother and a father all together.

After the first fortnight or three weeks of his absence, health, good humour and cheerfulness began to re-appear at Longbourn. Everything wore a happier aspect. The families who had been in town for the winter came back again, and summer finery and summer engagements arose. Mrs Bennet was restored to her usual querulous serenity, and by the middle of June Charles was so much recovered as to be able to enter Meryton without peevish outbursts of envy about Luke's good fortune. This event of such happy promise, Edward wrote to John, made him hope, that by the following Christmas, Charles might be so tolerably reasonable as to not mention the Militia above once a day, unless by some cruel and malicious arrangement at the war-office, another regiment should be quartered at Meryton.

The time fixed for John's northern tour was now fast approaching; and fortnight only of it was wanting, when a letter arrived from Mrs Gardiner which at once curtailed its commencement, and curtailed its extent. Mr Gardiner would be prevented by business from setting out till a fortnight later in July, and must be in London again within a month; and that left too short a period for them to go any further than Derbyshire, although John intended to stay on with Edward, while the Gardiners returned to London. In Derbyshire there was enough to be seen, to occupy the chief of their three weeks, and to Mrs Gardiner it had the peculiarly strong attraction of being a country where she had been very happy prior to her marriage. Edward, on receiving this news, was sympathetic, but happy that they were to visit and that John could extend his stay on the Fellowes's estate.

Mr Darcy was on his way back to Pemberley from Rosings,

where he had indeed been forwarding his match with Miss De Bourgh by making her an offer and securing the blessing of his aunt, Lady Catherine. The date was now set for the marriage to go ahead, and he was in an indulgent frame of mind; with schemes to fit up a very pretty sitting-room for his wife and his sister to share off a spacious lobby up stairs. It was pleasant to picture Mrs and Miss Darcy there together, and he was smiling as he cantered towards Pemblerley. Ahead was a carriage that he recognised as belonging to his neighbour, Fellowes, newly arrived in Derbyshire, and so he drew alongside to pay his respects to Mrs Fellowes, and to invite them to Pemberley now that he was returned.

To his astonishment, Edward Bennet was in the carriage, and Mr Fellowes begged leave to introduce Edward to Mr Darcy as his newly adopted son. Mr Darcy's surprize was great indeed, and he issued them a general invitation to visit at Pemberley if they were ever passing, "Miss Darcy will be pleased to see you, and there are some arriving tomorrow who will claim an acquaintance with you; Mr Bingley and his sisters."

Mrs Fellowes glanced at her husband and at Edward, and seeing in her husband, who was fond of society, a perfect willingness to accept, she ventured to engage for their attendance, and the day after next was fixed on.

They were received by Mr Darcy and Miss Darcy, with great cordiality, and by Mrs Hurst and Miss Bingley by a curtsey; Mr Hurst had managed to engage Mr Bingley and Mrs Annesley in cards, and did not even look up at their entrance, although both Mr Bingley and Mrs Annesley came forward to greet them politely, before resuming play.

Miss Bingley, in the imprudence of anger at seeing Edward, took the first opportunity of saying, with sneering civility,

"Pray, Mr Bennet, are not the – militia removed from Meryton? They must be a great loss to your family."

In Darcy's presence, she dared not mention Wickham's name,

but Edward instantly comprehended that he was uppermost in her thoughts; and exerting himself vigorously to repel the ill-natured attack, Edward presently answered the question in a tolerably disengaged tone. While he spoke, an involuntary glance shewed Darcy with a heightened complexion, and Miss Darcy overcome with confusion, and hardly able to lift her eyes. Had Miss Bingley known what pain she was then giving her beloved friend, she undoubtedly would have refrained from the hint; but she had merely intended to discompose Edward, by bringing attention to the follies and absurdities by which some part of his family were connected with that corps. Not a syllable had reached her of Miss Darcy's meditated elopement. To no creature had it been revealed, where secrecy was possible. Miss Darcy had told Edward, believing he needed to know before committing himself to her; but aside from her brother, and her guardian, Colonel Fitzpatrick, no body else knew.

Edward's collected behaviour, however, soon quieted Mr Darcy's fears; and as Miss Bingley, vexed and disappointed, dared not approach nearer to Wickham, Miss Darcy also recovered in time, though not enough to be able to speak any more. She was very conscious of Mr Edward Bennet Fellowes being in the room, but did not wish to draw attention to their understanding with any more than the civilities expected of her as hostess. Mrs Annesley gave her a significant look, and a smile, to remind her of her post, and she rang the bell for the servants to bring refreshments.

The attention of the company now turned to the next variation which their visit afforded, when servants came in with cold meat, cake, and a variety of all the finest fruits in season. There was now employment for the whole party, not just the card players; and the beautiful pyramids of grapes, nectarines, and peaches, soon collected all the ladies around the table. With this distraction absorbing the attention of the party, Edward now determined to speak to Mr Darcy, and hoped that Miss Darcy had dropt a hint of their attachment; but it appeared she had not, or that Mr Darcy had failed to notice the frequent mentions of 'Mr Fellowes' in her letters.

Mr Darcy expressed his approbation for Edward paying his addresses to Miss Darcy, but asked if he could relate an event in her recent past, which might cause him some pain. Edward assured Mr Darcy that his sister had related the whole, and that it was of no consequence to him, and could be completely forgot; which reassurance was most gratefully received, and it was all settled between them that Edward should make Miss Darcy an offer, although Darcy stipulated that her's was the final decision. They returned to the party, most of whom did not seem to have noticed their absence. Miss Darcy feared to meet Edward's eye; but he did manage to indicate silently to her that all had passed well in his going to her brother.

The visit did not continue long after the events above-mentioned, and Mr Darcy attended the Fellowes and Edward to their carriage with many assurances on both sides that they would all meet again soon, and Edward was able to relay the successful outcome of his visit and discussion with Mr Darcy. Mr and Mrs Fellowes were delighted, and looked forward to welcoming a new daughter as well as a son into their home, and with the hope of grand-children to come.

Chapter Twenty-three

Edward had been a good deal disappointed in not finding a letter from John since the last notification about the postponement of his visit; and this disappointment had been renewed on each successive morning, until the third. His repining was over, and John justified by the receipt of two letters at once, on one of which was marked that it had been missent elsewhere. Edward showed Mrs Fellowes, and she said she was not surprised at it, for John had written the direction remarkably ill.

They had just been preparing to walk when the letters came in; and Mr and Mrs Fellowes, leaving Edward to enjoy them in peace, set off by themselves. The one missent must be first attended to; it had been written longer ago. The beginning contained an account of all the little parties and engagements, with such news as the country afforded; plus reassurance that the northern tour would still go ahead, and he would be with Edward soon. But the latter half, which was dated a day after the beginning, and written in evident agitation, gave more important intelligence. It was to this effect:

"Since writing the above, dearest brother, something has occurred of a most unexpected and serious nature; but I am afraid of alarming you – be assured that we are all well. What I have to say relates to Luke. An express came at twelve last night, just as we were all gone to bed, from Colonel Forster to inform us that Luke was gone from his house, with one of his officers; to own the truth, with Wickham! Imagine our surprise. To Charles, however, it does not seem so wholly unexpected. I am very, very shocked; according to Colonel Forster's letter, there have been what I can only describe as intrigues extending into tradesmen's families; they are both owing money for goods and services rendered, and have gambling debts of honour against them. I am willing to hope the best, and that matters have been misunderstood, but it does look thoughtless to leave Brighton together in the middle of the night, without settling their debts first. Our poor mother is sadly grieved. My father bears it better. I am not so thankful now that we did not let them know what was said about Wickham; perhaps it was not for the best, but we were not to know. They were off Saturday night about twelve, as is conjectured, but were not missed until yesterday morning at eight. Luke left a few lines for Mrs Forster, but said nothing of whither they were bound, nor about the debts. I must conclude, for I cannot be long from my poor mother. I am afraid you will not be able to make it out, but I hardly know what I have written."

Without allowing himself time for consideration, and scarcely knowing what he felt, Edward, on finishing this letter, instantly seized the other, and opening it with the utmost impatience, read as follows: it had been written a day later than the conclusion of the first.

"By this time, my dearest brother, you have received my hurried letter; I wish this may be more intelligible, but though not confined by time, my head is so bewildered that I cannot answer for being coherent. Best of brothers, I hardly know what I would write, but I have bad news for you, and it cannot be delayed. Imprudent as it appears Wickham and Luke have been, we are now anxious to be assured that a claim by a tradesman's daughter is not true, but a doctor has confirmed she is with child. Luke's short letter to Mrs Forster gave her to understand that they were bound for Scotland, but something was dropped by Denny expressing his belief that Wickham never intended to go there, and Colonel Forster attempted to trace their route.

He did trace them easily to Clapham, but no farther; for on entering that place, they removed into a hackney-coach and dismissed the chaise that brought them from Epsom. All that is known after this is, that they were seen to continue the London road. I know not what to think. After making every possible enquiry on that side of London, Colonel F. came on into Hertfordshire, anxiously renewing them at all the turnpikes, and at the inns in Barnet and Hatfield, but without any success, no such people had been seen to pass through. With the kindest concern he came on to Longbourn, and broke his apprehensions to us in a manner most creditable to his heart. I am sincerely grieved for him and Mrs F. but no one can throw any blame on them. Our distress, my dear brother, is very great. My father and mother know not what to think, and neither do I; Colonel F. is not disposed to depend upon Wickham returning voluntarily to pay his debts and honour his obligations; and said that he feared Wickham was not a man to be trusted. My poor mother is really ill and keeps to her room. Could she exert herself it would be better, but this is not to be expected; and as to my father, I never in my life saw him so affected. Poor Charles has anger for having concealed their activities and schemes, but as it was a matter of confidence, one cannot wonder. I am truly glad, dear brother, that you have a new family now and have been spared these distressing scenes, but now that the first shock is over, shall I own that I wish you were here with us? I am not so selfish as to wish to ruin your new-found happiness, and to press for your return, if inconvenient to Mr and Mrs Fellowes. Adieu. I take up my pen again to do, what I have just told you I would not, but circumstances are such, that I cannot help earnestly wishing that you could come, as soon as possible. My father is going to London with Colonel Forster instantly, to try to discover them. What he means to do, I am sure I know not; but his excessive distress will not allow him to pursue any measure in the best and safest way, and Colonel Forster is obliged to be at Brighton again tomorrow evening. In such an exigence, I am hoping my uncle Gardiner will advise and assist my father; I rely upon his goodness."

"Oh! Where, where is Mr Fellowes?" cried Edward, darting from his seat as he finished the letter, in eagerness to follow him, without losing a moment of the time so precious; but as he reached the door, it was opened by a servant, and Mr Darcy followed him in to the room. Edward's pale face and impetuous manner made him start, but before he could recover himself to speak, Edward hastily exclaimed, "I beg your pardon, but I must leave you. I must find Mr Fellowes this moment, on business that cannot be delayed; I have not a moment to lose."

"Good God! What is the matter?" cried he, with more feeling than politeness; then recollecting himself, he called the servant back in, and instructed him to fetch his master and mistress home, instantly. The servant looked to Edward for confirmation, and Edward commissioned him, in so breathless an accent as to be almost unintelligible, to do as Mr Darcy commanded.

On his quitting the room, Edward collapsed onto a chair and buried his face in his hands. He looked so miserably ill that it was impossible for Darcy to leave, or refrain from saying in a tone of commiseration, "Is there nothing you can take for your immediate relief?" And seeing a bell, called another servant to bring a glass of wine.

Edward drank it and felt well enough to endeavour to explain. "I am quite well, I thank you. I am only distressed by some dreadful news from Longbourn. I have just had a letter from John; it cannot be concealed, my brother, Luke, has gone off with Wickham from Brighton to London. They have left behind debts, and worse; there is a tradesman's daughter, and a child on the way. Luke has no money, no connections; I do not know what he will do in London with someone like Wickham."

Darcy was fixed in astonishment.

"When I consider," Edward continued, jumping to his feet to walk about the room in a very agitated manner, "that I might have prevented it! I who knew what he was. Had I but explained some part of it only – some part of what I had learned from Miss Darcy, to my own family! Had his character been known, this could not have happened. But it is all, all too late now."

"I am grieved, indeed," cried Darcy, "grieved – shocked. But is it all certain, absolutely certain?"

"Oh yes! They left Brighton together, and were traced almost to London."

"And what has been done, what has been attempted to discover them?"

"My father, Mr Bennet, is gone to London to my uncle Gardiner, and John has written to beg my return; but I do not know whether Mr and Mrs Fellowes can spare me to go away again so soon."

Darcy shook his head in silent sympathy, as Edward continued berating himself,

"When my eyes were opened to his real character. Oh! Had I known what I ought, what I dared to do! But I knew not – I was afraid of doing too much. Wretched, wretched mistake!"

Darcy made no answer. He seemed scarcely to hear what Edward was saying. Edward observed and instantly understood it; Mr Darcy would not want his beloved sister allied with a family in the deepest disgrace, and then the humiliation and misery swallowed up even that private fear, and he sank back on to his chair with his head in his hands again.

There was a pause of several minutes before Mr Darcy spoke.

"I am afraid I have nothing to offer but real, though unavailing, concern. Would to heaven that any thing could be either said or done on my part, that might offer consolation or remedy for this situation. This unfortunate affair will, I fear, prevent my sister's having the pleasure of receiving you at Pemberley? I came with an express invitation from her to you and Mr and Mrs Fellowes."

"Please be so kind as to apologise to Miss Darcy. Say that urgent business calls me elsewhere. Conceal the unhappy truth as long as it is possible; I do not wish to distress her with tales of more of Wickham's infamies."

Darcy assured Edward of his secrecy, again expressed his sorrow for what had occurred, wished it a happier conclusion than there was at present reason to hope – perhaps the debts were not so great, perhaps the young woman was mistaken in her accusations – and leaving his compliments for Mr and Mrs Fellowes, he went away.

As he quitted the room, Edward felt how improbable it was that they would now become brothers, or see each other on terms of such cordiality as had marked the last few encounters. And how he would probably now lose Miss Darcy's regard, and all for Luke, who would neither know nor care about this outcome of his wild and ungoverned actions.

Chapter Twenty-four

Edward spent the time waiting for Mr and Mrs Fellowes's return in reviewing Luke's dealings with the –shire militia. He had never perceived, while the regiment was in Hertfordshire, that Luke had any but the most passing connection with Wickham; indeed Wickham was more in company with women than men, other than his fellow officers, and no-one had ever laid a charge of gaming against him as far as Edward knew. Indeed, there was nothing that Edward could call to mind that would have in any way indicated this outcome; Luke had spent his time with Charles, and Mrs Forster; Denny was a favourite, and other officers had occasionally been mentioned by name; but Wickham? When had that connection begun? It must have been at Brighton; oh! The mischief of neglect and mistaken indulgence towards such a son as Luke who needed far firmer guidance from his parents than he had ever received.

Edward was wild to be at Longbourn – to hear, to see, to be

upon the spot, to share with John in the cares that must now fall wholly upon him, in a family so deranged; a father absent, a mother incapable of exertion, and requiring constant attendance; and though almost persuaded that finding Luke would be as bad as never seeing him again, Edward was not convinced that his father and uncle Gardiner could do much to retrieve the situation, even should they find him. Mr and Mrs Fellowes had hurried back in alarm, supposing, by the servant's account, that their son had been taken suddenly ill; but satisfying them instantly on that head, he eagerly communicated the cause of their summons, letting Mr Fellowes read the letters out loud, as his own voice was trembling with shock.

Mr Fellowes said, "Of course you must go at once," and called the servant to order the carriage, and Edward's manservant to pack his bags. "You can be off in an hour. Do you wish us to accompany you? We need not trouble Mr and Mrs Bennet for a room; we can stay at our house in London after taking you to Longbourn."

"Oh!" cried Mrs Fellowes, "what about Pemberley? Miss Darcy? Daniels said that Mr Darcy was here when you sent for us; - was it so?"

"Yes, and I told him we would not be able to keep any engagements for the foreseeable future. I sent our apologies to Miss Darcy. That is all settled. And I would greatly appreciate your coming with me, if it is not too much trouble."

"That is all settled," repeated Mrs Fellowes to herself as she ran into her own room, calling for her maid to pack her bags, "and what of Miss Darcy? Will her brother disclose the truth? And what will that mean for poor Edward? What if she calls off the match? Oh, that I knew how it was!"

But wishes were in vain; or at best could serve only to amuse her as she sent for her housekeeper and issued instructions for their absence; not knowing how long it would be this time. The housekeeper took the instructions with perfect calm, and wished her mistress a good journey. An hour saw the whole completed; and nothing remained but to go. After all the misery of the morning, Edward found himself, and his adopted parents, in a shorter space of time than he could have supposed, seated in their carriage, and on the road to Longbourn.

"I have been thinking it over, Edward," said Mr Fellowes, as they drove from the town, "and really, upon serious consideration, I am inclined to judge that this may be as John says in his letter, not so very bad. I cannot imagine that Wickham would form a design against a girl of the lower classes, living close to the camp. Could he expect that her father would not step forward? Could he expect to be noticed again by the regiment, after such an affront? His temptation is not adequate to the risk."

"Do you really think so," cried Edward, brightening up for a moment.

"Upon my word," said Mrs Fellowes, "I begin to be of your father's opinion. It is really too great a violation of decency, honour, and interest for him to be guilty of it. I cannot think so very ill of Wickham. Can you, yourself, Edward, so wholly give him up, as to believe him capable of this?"

"Not perhaps of neglecting his own interest. But of every other neglect I can believe him capable. Although, I confess I did not know he was a gamer. But I dare not hope any thing."

"Gaming debts are simple to discharge," Mr Fellowes said easily, "I wonder he did not do so rather than choosing to leave."

"I do not believe him to have any money other than the army pay," said Edward.

"Perhaps his colonel will loan him enough to pay off his debts, and he may remain in the militia."

"I am not able to judge," said Edward.

"How could Luke have become so lost to every thing?" asked Mrs Fellowes.

"I know not what to say," Edward replied, with tears in his eyes, "Perhaps I am not doing him justice. But he is very young; he has never been taught to think on serious subjects; and for the last half year, nay, for a twelvemonth, he has been given up to nothing but amusement. He has been allowed to dispose of his time in the most idle manner, and to adopt any opinions that came in his way. Since the –shire were first quartered at Meryton, nothing but the army and officers, have been in his head. He has been doing everything in his power by thinking and talking on the subject, to give greater – what shall I call it? Susceptibility to his feelings and attachments, which are naturally lively enough. And I am afraid that I know that Wickham has every charm of person that can captivate any body, although I was not aware that he was a particular friend of Luke's when they left Meryton for Brighton. The mischief seems to have happened since they encamped there."

"Do you know some thing to Wickham's discredit, Edward?" asked Mr Fellowes.

"I regret that I do," said Edward. He gave them to understand, in as guarded a manner as he could; that by what Miss Darcy had told him, and what Mr Darcy had been about to corroborate, that Wickham's actions were not so amiable as they had been considered in Hertfordshire. In confirmation of this, he related the particulars of all the pecuniary transactions in which Wickham had been connected with the Darcys, without mentioning the intended elopement with Miss Darcy. Mrs Fellowes was surprised and concerned, "And do you really know all this?" she cried.

"I do indeed," replied Edward, "I have been told on the very best authority of his infamous behaviour towards Mr Darcy, and there are other circumstances, not at all to his credit, which I am not at liberty – which is it not worth while to relate; but his lies about the Pemberley family are endless. We all know them to be liberal and respectable, but the way Wickham talks of them, we were led to believe they behaved very basely indeed."

"But does Luke know nothing of this? How can he be ignorant of what you and John seem so well to understand?"

"Oh, yes! That – that is worst of all," cried Edward in some distress, "I only learned of this as the regiment was about to leave Meryton, and as that was the case, neither John, to whom I related the whole, nor I thought it not necessary to make our knowledge public; for what use could it apparently be to any one, that the good opinion which all the neighbourhood had of Wickham, should then be overthrown? And even when it was settled that Luke should go with the Forsters, the necessity of opening his eyes to Wickham's character never occurred to me, as there had been no previous relationship between them, as far as any body could tell. That Luke could be in any danger from an association with Wickham never entered my head. That such a consequence as this should ensue, you may easily believe was far enough from my thoughts."

"When they removed to Brighton, therefore, you had no reason, I suppose to believe them much in company with each other?"

"Not the slightest. Luke was a general favourite of the officers, or liked to believe that he was, at any rate. He often mentioned one or two by name, but he was always accompanied by Charles, and mostly in attendance on Mrs Forster, and there was no especial mention of Wickham at all."

It may easily be believed, that however little of novelty could be added to their fears, hopes, and conjectures, on this interesting subject, by its repeated discussion, no other could detain them from it for long, during the whole of the journey. From Edward's thoughts it was never absent. Fixed there by the keenest of all anguish, self-reproach, he could find no interval of ease of forgetfulness, unlike Mrs Fellowes, who soon fell asleep with the motion of the carriage, and Mr Fellowes leaned forward to speak quietly to Edward.

"I could not say so while Mrs Fellowes was awake," said he, "but this girl troubles me. If she lives near a military encampment, she may well have started life as a respectable trades-man's daughter; but what has she become since? It may not be necessary to pay her off, and Wickham can focus on clearing his debts."

They travelled as expeditiously as possible; and sleeping one night on the road, reached Longbourn by dinner-time the next day. It was a comfort to Edward to know that John could not have been wearied by long expectation.

Edward jumped out of the chaise, hurried into the vestibule, where John who came running down stairs from his mother's apartment, immediately met him. They embraced affection-ately, whilst tears filled the eyes of both, and Edward lost not a moment in asking whether any thing had been heard of the fugitives.

"Not yet," replied John.

"Is my father in town?"

"Yes, he went on Tuesday, as I wrote you word."

"And have you heard from him often?"

"We have only heard once. He wrote me a few lines on Wednes-day, to say that he had arrived in safety, and to give me his direc-tions, which I particularly begged him to do. He merely added, that he should not write again, till he had something of import-ance to mention, and that my uncle Gardiner had invited him to stay at their house so he could be of assistance in the search."

"And my mother – how is she? How are you all?"

"My mother is tolerably well, I trust; though her spirits are greatly shaken. She is up stairs, and will have great satisfaction in seeing you and greeting Mr and Mrs Fellowes. She does not yet leave her dressing room. Mark and Charles, thank Heaven! are quite well."

"But you – how are you?" cried Edward, "You look pale. How much you must have gone through."

John, however, assured him of being perfectly well; and their conversation which had been passing while Mr and Mrs Fellowes alighted and gave orders to the coachman, were now put an end to by the necessity of welcoming the visitors, and thanking them for bringing Edward, with alternate smiles and tears.

When they were all in the drawing room, the questions which Edward had already asked, were of course repeated by Mr and Mrs Fellowes, and they soon found John had no intelligence to give. The sanguine hope of good, however, which the benevolence of his heart suggested, had not yet deserted him. He still believed that it would all end well, and that every morning would bring some letter, either from Luke or his father, to explain their proceedings, and perhaps announce that it was all a joke, or an unfortunate misunderstanding.

Mr and Mrs Fellowes staid to a hasty dinner, at which Mrs Bennet did not appear, and afterwards departed with many good wishes to the whole family, an earnest desire that Edward should join them at their London house as soon as he felt able to leave the Bennets, and an open invitation for Mr Bennet to join them, so that he did not have to stay in lodgings. Edward undertook to pass the invitation on to his father, but supposed he was already staying with the Gardiners, and promised to come very soon to the London house to rejoin his new parents.

Mrs Bennet, to whose apartment John and Edward then repaired, after a few minutes conversation together received them exactly as might be expected; with tears and lamentations of regret, invectives against the villainous conduct of Wickham to have led her little boy astray, and complaints of her own sufferings and ill usage; blaming every body but the person to whose ill judging indulgence the errors of her son must be principally owing.

"If I had been able," said she, "to carry my point of going to Brighton, with all my family, this would not have happened. Poor Luke had no body to look out for him. Why did the Forsters ever let him go out of their sight? I am sure there was some very great neglect or other on their part, for he is not vicious, not the kind of boy to do such a thing, if he had been well looked after. I always thought they were very unfit to have charge of him; but I was overruled, as I always am. Poor dear child! And now here's Mr Bennet gone away, and I know he will fight Wickham, wherever he meets him, and then he will be killed, and what is to become of us all? I know you will be kind to us, my dear John, but I do not know what we shall do."

Her sons exclaimed against such terrific ideas; and Edward repeated that Mr Gardiner was also in town, and would assist Mr Bennet in ever endeavour to find Luke, if not Wickham.

"Do not give way to useless alarm, mama," said John, "though it is right to be prepared for the worst, there is no occasion to look on it as certain."

"Indeed," added Edward, "As Mr Fellowes said, it is but a week since they left Brighton. In a few days more we may gain some news of them; but do not let us give the matter over as lost. It may be that this is all a misunderstanding that can be easily cleared up. My father can come home with Mr and Mrs Fellowes to their house in London, or go to my uncle, and they can consult together what is best to be done."

"Oh! my dear," replied Mrs Bennet, "that is exactly what I could most wish for. Mr Fellowes is very good indeed. And my brother Gardiner; the three of them will be able to contrive it all, I am sure."

Edward and John recommended moderation to her, as well in her hopes as her fears, and after talking with her in this manner, they left her to vent all her feelings on the housekeeper, who attended, in the absence of her husband and sons.

Though her sons were persuaded that there was no real occasion for such seclusion from the family, they did not attempt to oppose it, for they knew that she had not prudence enough to hold her tongue before the servants, while they waited at table, and judged it better than one only of the household, and the one whom they could most trust, should comprehend all her fears and solicitude on the subject.

Chapter Twenty-five

In the drawing-room they were joined by Mark and Charles; the faces of both were tolerably calm; and no change was visible in either, except that the loss of his favourite brother, or the anger which he had himself incurred in the business, had given something more of fretfulness to the accents of Charles. As for Mark, he was master enough of himself to whisper to Edward with a countenance of grave reflection, soon after they were seated.

"This is a most unfortunate affair; and will probably be much talked of. But we must stem the tide of malice, and pour into the wounded bosoms of each other, the balm of brotherly consolation."

Edward lifted up his eyes in astonishment, but was too much tired and oppressed to make any reply. Mark, however, continued to console himself with such kind of moral extractions from the evil before them.

In the afternoon, John and Edward were able to be for half an hour by themselves; and Edward immediately availed himself of the opportunity of making many enquiries, which John was equally eager to satisfy. After joining in general lamentations over the dreadful sequel of this event, which Edmund considered as all but certain, and John could not assert to be wholly impossible; the former continued the subject, by saying,

"But tell me all and every thing about it which I have not already heard. Give me farther particulars. What did Colonel Forster say? Had they no apprehension of the gambling or their involvement with this girl before Wickham and Luke ran away? They must have seen them go out together for ever."

"Colonel Forster did own that he had seen Luke in Wickham's company at night, but there was nothing in their behaviour to give him any alarm. I am so grieved for him. His behaviour was attentive and kind to the utmost."

"And was Denny in their confidence? Did he know about their nocturnal activities? Had Colonel Forster seen Denny himself?"

"Yes, but when questioned by him, Denny denied knowing anything about their activities, and would not give his real opinion about whether the girl's complaint could be genuine. He had no idea that they would leave Brighton with their debts unpaid; they did not share their plans with him."

"And so no body knew any thing about what Luke and Wickham were doing, or what they intended once a complaint was made against them?"

"Charles has owned, with a very natural triumph on knowing more than the rest of us, that in Luke's last letter, he had mentioned such a step, saying that they had run into difficulties in Brighton, and would be leaving without telling any body. He promised to let Charles know where they went, but that was all."

"And did Colonel Forster appear to think ill of Wickham himself? Does he know his real character?"

"I must confess that he did not speak so well of Wickham as he formerly did. He believed him to be imprudent and extravagant, but not a gamester, nor a seducer. Of course, we know differently on that score. And it appears, that Wickham also left Meryton greatly in debt, and with rumours of seductions as well; but I hope this may be false."

"Oh, John, had we been less secret, and told what we knew of him, this could not have happened!"

"Perhaps it would have been better," replied his brother, "but to expose the former faults of any person, without knowing whether they had changed for the better or have learned from their former mistakes, seemed unjustifiable. We acted with the best intentions."

"Could Colonel Forster repeat the particulars of Luke's note to his wife?"

"He brought it with him for us to see."

John then took it from his pocket-book, and gave it to Edward. These were the contents:

"My dear Mrs Forster

You will laugh when you know that I am gone, and I cannot help laughing myself at your surprise tomorrow morning, as soon as I am missed. You need not send them word at Longbourn of my going, if you do not like it, for I will contact them myself once every thing has died down again. Do not pay any attention to the rumours; they are greatly exaggerated by people who wish us ill, and as for that Betsy; you know she's no better than she should be. Good bye, and my best respects to Colonel Forster. I hope you will drink to our good journey and future. Your affectionate friend, Luke Bennet."

"Oh, thoughtless, thoughtless Luke!" cried Edward, when he had finished it. "It seems he was aware that there was a scandal brewing, at least. My poor father! How he must have felt it!"

"I never saw any one so shocked. He could not speak a word for full ten minutes. My mother was taken ill immediately, and the whole house in such confusion."

"Oh! John," cried Edward, "was there a servant belonging to it, who did not know the whole story before the end of the day?"

"I do not know – I hope there was – but to be guarded at such a time, is very difficult. My mother was in hysterics, and though I endeavoured to give her every assistance in my power, I had to call for the assistance of her maid, so I may not have done as much as I might have! But the horror of it all almost took from me my faculties."

"Your attendance upon her, has been too much for you. You do not look well. Oh! That I had been with you, you have had every care and anxiety upon yourself alone. And now I cannot stay beyond tomorrow; I must join Mr and Mrs Fellowes in London, where, perhaps I may hear at first hand what is happening. I will visit my uncle and aunt, and see my father; may be I can help with the search in some way."

"Mark and Charles have been very kind, and would have shared in every fatigue, I am sure, but I did not think it right for either of them. Mark is at work long hours, and studies so much as well, that his hours of repose should not be broken into. Charles is slight and delicate, and not suited to prolonged exertion. My aunt Philips came to Longbourn on Tuesday, after my father went away; and was so good as to stay till Thursday with me. She was of great use and comfort to our mother with her knowledge of nursing, and Lady Lucas has been very kind; she walked here on Wednesday morning to condole with us, and offered her services, or any of her daughters, if they could be of any use to us. Maria, especially, has been most attentive and helpful, with managing the servants, and ordering meals, whilst my mother is unable to do so."

"Lady Lucas had better have stayed at home," cried Edward, "perhaps she meant well, but, under such a misfortune as this, one cannot see too little of one's neighbours. Assistance is impossible! Condolence, insufferable. Let them triumph over us at a distance, and be satisfied."

"Nay, Edward, this is too unkind," John protested, "And I cannot do without Maria. She is here now, in the kitchen with Hill."

A suspicion darted into his brother's mind, but now was not the time to question whether John's present reliance on Maria Lucas was setting a precedent for their future relationship; instead, he proceeded to enquire into the measures which his father had meant to pursue, while in town, for the discovery of his errant son.

"He meant, I believe" replied John, "to go to Epsom, the place where they last changed horses, see the postilions, and try if any thing could be made out from them. His principal object must be, to discover the number of the hackney-coach which took them from Clapham. It had come with a fare from London; and as he thought the circumstances might be remarked, he meant to make enquiries at Clapham. If he could any how discover at what house the coachman had before set down his fare, he determined to make enquiries there, and hoped it might not be impossible to find out the stand and number of the coach. I do not know of any other designs that he had formed; but he was in such a hurry to be gone, and his spirits so greatly discomposed, that I had difficulty in finding out even so much as this."

Chapter Twenty-six

The whole family were in hopes of a letter from Mr Bennet the next morning, but the post came in without bringing a single line from him, or from Mr Gardiner. His family knew him to be on all common occasions, a most negligent and dilatory correspondent, but at such a time, they had hoped for exertion. They were forced to conclude, that he had no pleasing intelligence to send, but even of that they would have been glad to certain. Edward had waited only for the letters before he set off to join Mr and Mrs Fellowes in London.

When Edward was gone, John was certain at least of receiving constant information of what was going on, and Edward had promised, at parting, to prevail on his father to return to Longbourn, as soon as he could, and leave the search to Mr Gardiner and Mr Fellowes. This was to the great consolation of Mrs Bennet, who considered it the only security for her husband's not being killed in a duel.

Maria Lucas came early each day to Longbourn, and shared in John's attendance on Mrs Bennet, and was a great comfort to him, in his hours of freedom, during which it was clear to both of them that they were entering into an understanding. However, John did not want to speak with Luke's disgrace hanging over the whole family, while Maria did not care one jot about that, and did her best to communicate thus to John. His other aunt also visited them frequently, and always, as she said, with the design of cheering and heartening them up, though as she never came without reporting some fresh instance of Wickham's extravagance or irregularity, she seldom went away without leaving them more dispirited than she found them.

All Meryton seemed striving to blacken the man, who, but three months before, had been almost an angel of light. As John reported to Edward by letter; Wickham was declared to be in debt to every tradesman in the place, and his intrigues, all honoured with the title of seduction, had been extended into every tradesman's family, although no specific complaints had been raised. Every body declared that he was the wickedest young man in the world; and every body began to find out, that they had always distrusted the appearance of his goodness.

Edward, though he did not credit above half of the reports, still believed enough to make the more specific intelligence from Brighton more credible and persuasive.

John, who believed still less of it, became almost hopeless in the face of the accumulating evidence of Wickham's infamy. As soon as Edward reached the Fellowes' town house, he sent a servant to his uncle, and was delighted to find that Mr Bennet had been staying there, but was now gone back to Longbourn. Rendered spiritless by the ill-success of his endeavours, he had yielded to his brother-in-law's intreaty that he would return to his family, and leave it to him to do, whatever occasion might suggest to be advisable for continuing their pursuit.

Mr Gardiner reported that Mr Bennet had been to Epsom and Clapham, before his arrival into London, but without gaining any satisfactory extra information; and that he had also enquired of all the military barracks, and principal hotels in case they had gone to one of them, on their first coming to London, before they procured lodgings.

Mr Gardiner had also written on his note, "I have written to Colonel Forster to desire him to find out, if possible, from some of the young men's intimates in the regiment, whether Wickham has any relations or connections, who would be likely to know in what part of town he might seek to conceal himself. If there were any one, that one could apply to, with a probability of gaining such a clue as that, it might be of essential consequence. At present we have nothing to guide us. Colonel Forster will, I dare say, do every thing in his power to help us with any information."

Edward passed on this note under cover in a letter to John, and added, "I never heard of his having had any relations, except a father and mother, both of whom had been dead many years. It is possible, however, that some of his companions in the –shire, might be able to give more information; and though I am not very sanguine in expecting it, the application to Colonel Forster by my uncle, is something to look forward to. Please reassure my mother that my father is on his way back to Longbourn."

When Mrs Bennet was told of this good news, she did not express as much satisfaction as John had expected, considering what her anxiety for his life had been before.

"What? Is he coming back, and without Luke?" she cried, "Who is to fight Wickham, if he comes away?"

John endeavoured to explain that there was no need for Mr Bennet to fight Wickham or any body else, but Mrs Bennet could not attend – her beloved youngest son was still missing, and her husband was to come back without him!

Every day at Longbourn was now a day of anxiety; but the most anxious part of each was when the post was expected, or when Mr Bennet might be reasonably expected to arrive home. The arrival of letters was the first grand object of every morning's impatience. Through letters, whatever of good or bad was to be told, would be communicated, and every succeeding day was expected to bring some news of importance.

When Mr Bennet arrived, he had all the appearance of his usual philosophic composure. He said as little as he had ever been in the habit of saying; made no mention of the business that had taken him away, and it was some time before John had the courage to speak of it, or to give him a letter from Mr Collins which had arrived during his absence.

It was the afternoon, when he joined his remaining sons at tea, that John ventured to introduce the subject; and then, on his briefly expressing his sorrow for what he must have endured, his father replied, "Say nothing of that. Who should suffer it but myself? It has been my own doing, and I ought to feel it."

"You must not be too severe on yourself," replied John, "no body knew that any thing like this might happen."

"You may well warn me against such an evil as severity. Human nature is so prone to fall into it! No, John, let me once in my life feel how much I have been to blame. I am not afraid of being overpowered by the impression. It will pass away soon enough. And I have the pleasure of a letter from Mr Collins to brighten my day."

"Do you suppose them to be in London?"

"Yes; where else can they be so well concealed?"

"Luke always wanted to go to London," added Charles.

"He is happy then," said his father, dryly, "and his residence there will probably be of some duration, but little honour or income."

After a short silence, Mr Bennet said, "Well, well, let me look at this letter. Should you like the hear the contents, Mark? I know you always valued Mr Collins's stile of composition."

They were interrupted before he could open the letter, by Mrs Bennet's maid, who came to fetch her mistress's tea.

After she was gone with the tray, Mr Bennet cried, "This is a parade which does one good; it gives such an elegance to misfortune! Another day I will do the same; I will sit in my library, in my night cap and powdering gown, and give as much trouble as I can – or, perhaps, I may defer it until Charlie runs away."

"I am not going to run away, Papa," said Charles, fretfully, "if I should ever go to Brighton, I would behave much better than Luke."

"You go to Brighton! I would not trust you so near it as East Bourne, for fifty pounds! No, Charles, I have at last learnt to be cautious, and you will feel the effects of it. Tomorrow we look for a tutor to resume your studies, and then you will be entered at Oxford, and a suitable living sought for you in due course.

Until then, you are never to stir out of doors, until you can prove, that you have spent ten minutes of every day in a rational manner."

Charles was unsure how much of these pronouncements and threats were serious, and looked to John in confusion; but Mr Bennet's mind was made up. This remaining son of his must be placed securely, and respectably in the world, and as the son of a gentleman, there were few avenues available for Charles. He was not robust as Luke for the army, and now too old to be entered into the Navy; a clergyman he would become.

"How shall you like making sermons?" Mark asked his brother, "I should have liked it of all things."

"I cannot tell you," Charles replied, "but if it is to be part of my duty, the exertion will soon seem nothing."

Having settled Charles's future, Mr Bennet turned now to the letter from Mr Collins. "It wanted only this," said he, "to make my home-coming complete."

John, who knew what curiosities Mr Collins's letters always were, looked over his father's shoulder and read as follows:

My dear Sir,

I feel myself called upon, by our connection, and my situation in life, to condole with you on the grievous affliction you are now suffering under, of which we were yesterday informed by a letter from Hertfordshire. Be assured, my dear Sir, that Mrs Collins and myself sincerely sympathise with you, and all your respectable family, in your present distress, which must be of the bitterest kind. No arguments shall be wanting on my part, that can alleviate so severe a misfortune; or that may comfort you, under a circumstance that must be most afflicting to a parent's mind.

The death of your son would have been a blessing in comparison with finding that he has turned out so vicious and unprincipled. And it is all the more to be lamented, because there is reason to suppose, as my dear Charlotte informs me, that this licentiousness of behaviour has proceeded from a faulty degree of indulgence, though, at the same time, for the consolation of yourself and Mrs Bennet, I am inclined to believe that his own disposition must be naturally bad, or he could not be guilty of such enormities, at so early an age.

Howsoever that may be, you are grievously to be pitied, in which opinion I am not only joined by Mrs Collins, but likewise by Lady Catherine, and her daughter, to whom I have related the affair. Let me pass on Lady Catherine's advice, given so condescendingly, that you throw off your unworthy child from your affection for ever, and leave him to reap the fruit of his own heinous offences. I am, dear Sir, etc, etc.

Edward did not write again until he had been in conference with his uncle Gardiner, on that gentleman's receiving a letter from Colonel Forster; and then he had nothing of a pleasant nature to send. It was not known that Wickham had a single relation, with whom he kept up any connection, and it was certain he had no near one living. His former acquaintance had been numerous; but since he had been in the militia, it did not appear that he was on terms of particular friendship with any of them. There was no one therefore who could be pointed out, as likely to give any news of him. And in the wretched state of his own finances, there was the very powerful motive for secrecy in the discovery that he really had left gaming debts behind him, to a very considerable amount; these debts of honour were formidable. Colonel Forster believed that more than a thousand pounds would be necessary to clear his expences at Brighton, and that was without settling with 'Betsy'; who was still claiming to be with child. Mr Gardiner did not attempt to conceal these particulars from Edward, who passed them on to his family at Longbourn.

And, as for Edward himself, it was not thought appropriate by either his uncle, nor his adopted parents, that he should involve himself personally in the search; and as Mr Fellowes wished to shield his wife from the more distressing particulars, they returned to Frithton Court, leaving the search to Mr Gardiner, and, had they but known it; Mr Darcy.

Chapter Twenty-seven

Two days after Mr Bennet's return, as John and Maria were walking together in the shrubbery behind the house, they saw the housekeeper coming towards them, and, concluding that she came to call them to Mrs Bennet, went forward to meet her; but instead of the expected summons, she said to John, "I beg your pardon, sir, for interrupting you, but I was in hopes you might have got some good news from town, so I took the liberty of coming to ask."

"What do you mean, Hill?" cried Maria, "We have heard nothing from town, have we, John?"

"No indeed," John replied.

"Dear madam," cried Mrs Hill, in great astonishment, "don't you know there's been an express come for master from Mr Gardiner? He has been here this half hour, and master has had a letter."

Away ran John and Maria, too eager to get in to have time for speech. They ran through the vestibule into the breakfast room; from thence to the library; Mr Bennet was in neither, and they were on the point of seeking him upstairs with his wife, when they were met by the butler, who said, "If you are looking for my master, sir, he is walking towards the little copse."

"You go to him, John," Maria said, and he instantly passed through the hall once more, and ran across the lawn after his father, who was deliberately pursuing his way towards a small wood on one side of the paddock.

Panting with breath, John caught up with him, and eagerly cried out,

"Oh, Papa, what news? What news? Have you heard from my uncle?"

"Yes, I have had a letter from him by express."

"Well, and what news does it bring? Good or bad?"

"What is there of good to be expected?" said he, taking the letter from his pocket; "but perhaps you would like to read it."

John impatiently caught it from his hand.

"Read it aloud," said his father, "for I hardly know myself what it is about."

"Gracechurch-street, Monday, August 2

My dear brother,

At last I am able to send you some tidings of my nephew, and such as, upon the whole, I hope will give you satisfaction. Soon after you left me on Saturday, I was fortunate enough to find out in what part of London they were. The particulars, I reserve till we meet. It is enough to know they are discovered; I have seen them both, and if you are willing to perform the engagements which I have ventured to make on your side, I hope it will not be long before all is settled and forgotten. All that is required of you is, to assure to your son his equal share of the five thousand pounds secured among your children after the decease of yourself and my sister; and, moreover to enter into an engagement of allowing him, during your life, one hundred pounds per annum. These are conditions, which, considering every thing, I had no hesitation in complying with, as far as I thought myself privileged for you.

I shall send this by express, that no time may be lost in bringing me your answer. Colonel Forster interviewed the young woman, whose name is Elizabeth Cranshaw, and she has identified Luke, not Mr Wickham as her seducer. She is, according to Colonel Forster, of a very respectable family, which supplies washing services to the camp; and arrangements have been made to bring her to London, where she and Luke will be married. As for Mr Wickham, his circumstances are not so hopeless as they are generally believed to be. The world has been deceived in that respect; and I am happy to say that all his debts are to be discharged, and a commission purchased for him in a northern regiment. Luke has also expressed a desire to enlist, and so a commission will be purchased for him too, in a different militia regiment. If, as I conclude will be the case, you send me full powers to act in your name, throughout this whole business, I will immediately give direction to Haggerston for preparing a proper settlement on Miss Cranshaw, and to purchasing the commission for Luke in the militia.

There will not be the smallest occasion for your coming to town again; therefore, stay quietly at Longbourn, and depend upon my diligence and care. Send back your answer as soon as you can, and be careful to write explicitly. We have judged it best that Miss Cranshaw and Luke be married from this house, of which I hope you will approve. She comes to us today, and Luke tomorrow; and Mrs Gardiner will chaperone them both. I shall write again as soon as any thing more is determined. Your's, etc.

Edw. Gardiner"

"Is it possible?" cried John, "That Luke is to marry a washerwoman? But at least Wickham is not so undeserving as we have thought him, and has money enough to discharge his debts and buy into another commission. Have you answered this letter?"

"No; but it must be done soon."

Most earnestly did John then intreat him to lose no more time before he wrote.

"Let me write it for you," said John, "If you dislike the trouble yourself."

"I dislike it very much," he replied; "but it must be done."

And so saying, he turned back with John, and walked towards

the house.

"The terms, I suppose, must be complied with?"

"Complied with! Yes, yes, they must marry. There is nothing else to be done, however much we may regret our new daughter. But there are two things that I want very much to know; - one is, how much money your uncle has laid down, to bring this about; and the other, how I am ever to pay him."

"Money! My uncle!" cried John, "What do you mean, sir?"

"I mean that there is considerable expence in discharging Luke's debts, in arranging the marriage, buying the commission; and I do not believe that Wickham has money of his own; I suspect my brother of putting up the money to clear his debts as well, and of buying him the commission."

"That had not occurred to me," said John, "His debts to be discharged, and something still to remain! Oh! It must be my uncle's doings! Generous, good man, I am afraid he has distressed himself. A small sum could not do all this."

"No," said his father, "I think it will have cost no less than ten thousand pounds."

"Ten thousand pounds! Heaven forbid! How is half such a sum to be repaid?"

Mr Bennet made no answer, and each of them, deep in thought, continued silent till they reached the house. Their father then went to the library to write, and John sought out Maria in the kitchen, and asked her to come to the breakfast room, where he told her what was the outcome of the express letter to Mr Bennet.

"And Luke is to be married!" cried Maria, "How strange this is! And for this we are to be thankful? Small will be their chance of happiness, I think; such a mismatch of position and fortune."

"I comfort myself by thinking that there must be some affection in the case; Luke would not marry this Miss Cranshaw if he had not some regard for her. Though our kind uncle has done something toward clearing him, I cannot believe that ten thousand pounds or any thing like it, has been advanced. He has children of his own, and may have more. How could he spare even half ten thousand pounds?"

It now occurred to Maria, that Mrs Bennet was in all likelihood perfectly ignorant of what had happened; she went home, and John went to the library and asked his father, whether he would want him to make it known to her. He was writing, and without raising his head, coolly replied,

"Just as you please."

"May I take my uncle's letter to read to her?"

"Take whatever you like, and get away."

John took the letter from his writing table, and went up the stairs to Mrs Bennet's apartment. Mark and Charles were both with her: one communication would, therefore, do for all. After a slight preparation for good news, the letter was read aloud. Mrs Bennet could hardly contain herself. As soon as John had read Mr Gardiner's hope of Luke's being soon married, her joy burst forth and every following sentence did not diminish her jubilation. She was now in an irritation as violent from delight, as she had ever been fidgety from alarm and vexation. To know that her beloved son was to marry, and she would have a daughter, was enough. She was disturbed by no fear for Luke's felicity, nor humbled by any mention of his misconduct.

"My dear, dear Luke!" she cried, "This is delightful indeed! He will be married, and a baby on the way! I shall see him again! He will be married at sixteen! My good, kind brother! I knew how it would be – I knew he would manage every thing. But the clothes, the wedding clothes for my new daughter! She will need gown, cloaks, shoes. I will write to my sister Gardiner about them directly. Charles, my dear, run down to your father and ask him how much he will give her. Stay, stay, I will go myself. Ring the bell, Mark, for Hill. I will put on my things in a moment. My dear, dear Luke! How merry we shall all be together when we meet! And to have a baby in the house again!"

John endeavoured to give some relief to the violence of these transports, by leading her thoughts to the obligations which Mr Gardiner's behaviour laid them all under.

"For we must attribute this happy conclusion," he added, "in a great measure, to his kindness. We are persuaded that he has pledged himself to assist Luke with money."

"Well," cried his mother, "it is all very right; who should do it but her own uncle? If he had not had a family of his own, I and my children must have had all his money you know, and it is the first time we have ever had any thing from him, except a few presents. Well! I am so happy! In a short time, I shall have a son married, and a daughter, and a grand-child! My dear John, I am in such a flutter, that I am sure I can't write; so I will dictate and Mark can write for me, he has a clear hand. We will settle with your father about the money afterwards; but the things should be ordered immediately."

She was then proceeding to all the particulars of calico, muslin, and cambric, and would shortly have dictated some very plentiful orders, had not John, though with some difficulty, persuaded her to wait, till her husband was at leisure to be consulted. One day's delay would be of small importance; and Mrs Bennet was too happy, to be quite so obstinate as usual. Other schemes too came into her head.

"I will go to Meryton," said she, "as soon as I am dressed, and tell the good, good news to my sister Philips. And as I come back, I can call on Lady Lucas and Mrs Long. Charles, run down and order the carriage. An airing would do me a great deal of good, I am sure. Can I do anything for any one in Meryton? Oh, here comes Hill. My dear Hill, have you heard the good news? Master Luke is to be married; and you shall all have a bowl of punch, to make merry at the wedding."

Mrs Hill began instantly to express her joy. John received his share of congratulations among the rest, and then, sick of all this folly, took refuge in his own room, so that he might think with freedom. He wondered what Maria might think of having a washerwoman as a sister-in-law; and it struck him that Mr Darcy may not allow his sister to ally herself to a family whose youngest son had sunk so low, either.

Putting these concerns aside; John wrote to Edward as he had promised: detailing the contents of the letter from Mr Gardiner, and ending with,

"If we are ever to learn what Luke's and Wickham's debts have been, and how much is settled on Miss Cranshaw, we shall know exactly what my uncle has done for them, because Wickham has not a sixpence of his own, of that we were certain. The kindness of my uncle and aunt can never be requited. Their taking Miss Cranshaw into their home, and affording her their personal protection and countenance ahead of her marriage, is such a sacrifice to her advantage, as years of gratitude cannot enough acknowledge. By this time, Luke and Miss Cranshaw (I suppose I will have to become accustomed to calling her 'Elizabeth' or 'Betsy', as she is to be my sister), are actually with my uncle and aunt in Gracechurch-street! If such goodness does not make Luke behave, I do not know what will. We must now endeavour to forget all that has passed on either side. I hope and trust that they will be happy married, and that their mutual affection will steady them. I flatter myself that they will settle so quietly in the militia camp, and live in so rational a manner, as may in time make their past prudence forgotten. And as for Mr Wickham; I hope he will go to his new regiment in the north country, and make a change for the best at last. Finally, my dearest brother, although I can only hope for rational happiness and worldly prosperity for my youngest brother and his new wife, when I look back on what we had feared, I feel all the advantages of what we have gained."

Chapter Twenty-eight

Mr Bennet had very often wished, before this period of his life, that, instead of spending his whole income, he had laid by an annual sum, for the better provision of his children, and of his wife, if she survived him. He now wished it more than ever. Had he done his duty in that respect, Luke need not have been indebted to his uncle for whatever honour or credit could now be purchased for him. The satisfaction in gaining a washer-woman's daughter as a wife for his youngest son, might then have rested in its proper place. He was seriously concerned, that a cause of so little advantage to any one except Miss Cranshaw, should be forwarded at the sole expence of his brother-in-law, and he was determined, if possible, to find out the extent of his assistance, and to discharge the obligation as soon as he could.

When first Mr Bennet had married, economy was held to be perfectly useless; for, of course, they were to have a son. This son was to join in cutting off the entail, as soon as he should be of age, and the widow and younger children would be by that means be provided for. The son had duly arrived, as had the following four; but by then it was too late to be saving any way. Mrs Bennet had no turn for economy, and her husband's love of independence had alone prevented their exceeding their income.

Five thousand pounds was settled by marriage articles on Mrs Bennet and her children. But in what proportions it should be divided amongst the latter, depended on the will of the parents. This was one point, with regard to Luke at least, which was now to be settled, and Mr Bennet could have no hesitation in acceding to the proposal before him. In terms of grateful acknowledgement for the kindness of his brother, though expressed most concisely, he then delivered on paper his perfect approbation of all that was done, and his willingness to fulfil the engagements that had been made for him. He had never supposed that this scandal could be hushed up with so little inconvenience to himself. He would scarcely be ten pounds a-year the loser, by the hundred that was to be paid them; for, what with Luke's board and pocket allowance, and the continual presents in money, which passed to him, through his mother's hands, Luke's expences had been very little within that sum.

That it would be done with such trifling exertion on his side, too, was another very welcome surprise; for his chief wish at present, was to have as little trouble in the business as possible. When the first transports of rage which had produced his activity in seeking Luke were over, he naturally returned to all his former indolence. His letter was soon dispatched; for though dilatory in undertaking business, he was quick in its execution. He begged to know further particulars of what he was indebted to his brother; but he was too angry with Luke to send any message to him or his bride-to-be.

The good news quickly spread through the house; and with proportionate speed through the neighbourhood; though exact information about the bride's parentage and condition, was not amongst the information available to the gossips. It was borne in the neighbourhood with decent philosophy. To be sure it would have been more for the advantage of conversation, had Master Luke Bennet been transported, but there was much to be talked of in marrying him; and the good-natured wishes for his well-doing, which had proceeded before, from all the spiteful old ladies in Meryton, lost little of their spirit in this change of circumstances, because with little income, no expectations, and a baby a year to provide for; his misery was considered certain.

It was a fortnight since Mrs Bennet had been down stairs, but on this happy day, she again took her seat at the head of her table, and in spirits oppressively high. No sentiment of shame gave a damp to her triumph. Her conversation ran wholly on those attendants of elegant nuptials, fine muslins, new carriages and servants. She was busily searching through the neighbourhood for a proper situation for her son and daughter, and, without knowing or considering what their income might be, rejected many as deficient in size and importance.

"Haye-Park might do," said she, "if the Gouldings would quit it, or the great house at Stoke, if the drawing-room were larger; but Ashworth is too far off! I could not bear to have them ten miles from me; and as for Purvis Lodge, the attics are dreadful."

Her husband allowed her to talk without interruption, while the servants remained. But when they had withdrawn, he said to her, "Mrs Bennet, before you take any, or all of these houses for your son and daughter, let us come to a right understanding. Into one house in this neighbourhood, they shall never have admittance. I will not encourage the imprudence of our son, nor countenance his wife, by receiving them at Longbourn."

A long dispute followed this declaration; but Mr Bennet was firm: it soon led to another, and Mrs Bennet found, with amazement and horror, that her husband would not advance a guinea to buy clothes for his new daughter, and it could be certain that her family could do nothing for her. He protested that Luke should receive from him no mark of affection, whatever the occasion. Mrs Bennet could hardly comprehend it. That his anger could be carried to such a point of inconceivable resentment, as to refuse his new daughter a privilege, without which her marriage would scarcely seem valid, exceeded all that she could believe possible. She was more alive to the disgrace, which the want of new clothes must reflect on her daughter's nuptials, than to any sense of shame at the events which had brought about this marriage.

John was now most heartily sorry that Maria had been present at the disclosure of these unfavourable event, and that Edward had been forced to tell Mr Darcy about it too – for it now looked as though they might hope to conceal the beginnings, from all those who were not immediately on the spot. He had no fear of its spreading farther, through either Maria, nor Mr Darcy. But his heart grieved for Edward; there were few people on whose secrecy he would have more confidently depended; but at the same time, there was no one, whose knowledge of a brother's licentiousness, causing the fall of a young defenceless woman, might not make question their own connection with such a family. This might cause a gulf to open up between Edward and Miss Darcy too; and for that, John was truly sorry. He could not see how Mr Darcy could connect himself with the Bennet family now, even though Edward was nominally of the Fellowes family; the connection between the two families was easy to decipher. It may not matter quite so much to Sir William and Lady Lucas, who could give Maria nothing on her marriage; but could Mr Darcy ally his family to that of a washerwoman's?

How Luke and Betsy were to be supported in tolerable independence, he could not imagine. But how little of permanent happiness could belong to a couple who were only brought together because his passions were stronger than her virtue?

Mr Gardiner soon wrote again to his brother.

To Mr Bennet's acknowledgements he briefly replied, with assurances of his eagerness to promote the welfare of any of his family; and concluded with intreaties that the subject might never be mentioned to him again. The principal purport of his letter was to inform them that Mr Wickham had gone North to an ensigncy in General –'s regiment. He added that he had written to Colonel Forster, to inform him of the arrangements for the wedding and to request that he would satisfy the various creditors in and near Brighton, with assurances of speedy payment, for which he had pledged himself. He requested Mr Bennet would give himself the trouble of carrying similar assurances to any of Luke's creditors in Meryton. He believed Luke had given in all his debts; Haggerston had the directions, and all would be completed in a week. The newly-married couple would then travel to Brighton to rejoin the militia there, unless they were first invited to Longbourn.

Mr Bennet and John saw all the advantages of Wickham's removal to a far regiment, and of Luke and his wife returning to Brighton, as well as Mr Gardiner could do. But Mrs Bennet was not so well pleased with it. Luke's being settled in Brighton, when she had expected most pleasure and pride in their company, for she had by no means given up her plan of their residing in Hertfordshire, was a severe disappointment.

Mr Bennet firmly refused to allow Luke and his wife to come to Longbourn before going to Brighton, but John in person, and Edward by letter, urged him so earnestly, yet so rationally and mildly, to receive them at Longbourn as soon as they were married, that he was prevailed upon to think as they thought, and act as they wished. And their mother had the satisfaction of knowing, that she would be able to shew her married son and daughter-in-law in the neighbourhood, before they were banished back to Brighton. When Mr Bennet wrote again to his brother, therefore, he sent his permission for them to come; and it was settled, that as soon as the ceremony was over, they should proceed to Longbourn.

Chapter Twenty-nine

Luke's wedding day arrived, and John felt for him, certainly more than he felt for himself. The carriage was sent to meet the newly-weds at --, and they were to return in it by dinner-time. Their arrival was dreaded by his eldest brother, who gave Luke the feeling which would have attended himself, had he been the culprit, and was therefore wretched in the thought of what Luke must be enduring.

They came. The family was assembled in the breakfast room, to receive them. Smiles decked the face of Mrs Bennet, as the carriage drove up to the door; her husband looked impenetrably grave; her sons alarmed, anxious, uneasy.

Luke's voice was heard in the vestibule, booming a greeting to the butler, the door was thrown open and he was in the room. Mrs Bennet stepped forward, embraced Luke, and welcomed him with rapture; gave her hand with an affectionate smile to the young woman who bounced past Luke to greet her new mother, and wished them both joy, with an alacrity which shewed no doubt of their happiness.

Their reception from Mr Bennet, to whom Luke then turned to introduce Betsy, was not quite so cordial. His countenance rather gained in austerity; and he scarcely opened his lips; acknowledging his son's wife with a slight bow. John was shocked. Luke was Luke still; untamed, unabashed, wild, noisy, and fearless, and it appeared that Betsy was cut from the same cloth. They turned from brother to brother, demanding their congratulations, and when at length they all sat down, Luke looked eagerly round the room, pointed out to Betsy some little alteration in it, and observed, with a laugh, that it was a great while since he had been here. Betsy remarked that it must be a most inconvenient sitting room for the evening, in summer; as the windows were full west.

Mrs Bennet assured her they never sat there after dinner; but John was shocked again at such easy self-assurance, and observed them with some pain, as they behaved as though they had neither of them done any thing amiss. There was no want of discourse. Luke and his mother could neither of them talk fast enough, and Betsy interjected, corrected Luke's assertions, and both of them seemed to have the happiest memories in the world. Nothing of the past was recollected with pain; and Luke led voluntarily to subjects, which his brothers would not have alluded to for the world.

"Only think of its being three months," he cried, "since I went away; it seems but a fortnight, I declare; and yet there have been things enough happened in the time. Good gracious! When I went away, I am sure I had no more idea of being married till I came back again! Though I thought it would be very good fun if I was."

Betsy laughed heartily. Mr Bennet lifted up his eyes. John looked expressively at Luke; but he, who never saw nor heard anything of what he chose to be insensible, gaily continued, "Oh! Mama, do the people here abouts know I am married to-day? I was afraid they might not; and we overtook William Goulding in his curricle, so I was determined he should know it, and so I let down the side glass next to him, and made Betsy take off her glove, and put her hand upon the window frame, so that he might see the ring, and then we both bowed and smiled like any thing."

John could bear it no longer. He got up and left the room; and returned no more, till he heard them passing through the hall to the dining parlour. He could hear Betsy exclaiming as Mr Bennet offered her his arm, and commenting to Luke, how fancy it was to have a separate room for eating in! John joined them in time for Luke to say, "Ah! John, I take your place now, and you must go lower, because I am a married man."

It was not to be supposed that time would give Luke that embarrassment from which he had been so wholly free at last. His ease and good spirits increased, and he seemed proud to be able to claim such a woman as his wife. He longed to see Mrs Philips, the Lucases, and their other neighbours, and to hear Betsy called, 'Mrs Bennet', by each of them; and in the mean time, he took Betsy after dinner to shew the ring, and boast of being married, to Mrs Hill and the two housemaids.

"Well, mama," said he, when they were all returned to the breakfast room, while Betsy went up to her room to rest, "what think you of my bride? Is she not charming? I am sure my brothers must all envy me. I only hope that they may have half my good luck. They must all go to Brighton. That is the place for good wives. What a pity it is, mama, we did not all go."

"Very true; and if I had my will, we should. But my dear Luke, I don't like at all your going back to Brighton without us. Must it be so?"

"Oh, lord! Yes; there is nothing to that. I shall like it of all things, and Betsy's parents are there, you know. You and papa, and my brothers, must come down and see us. We shall be at Brighton all the winter, and I dare say there will be some balls, and I will take care to get good partners for you all."

"I should like it beyond any thing!" said his mother.

"And then when you go away, you may leave one or two of my brothers behind you; and I dare say I shall get wives for them before the winter is over."

"I thank you for my share of the favour," said Mark, stiffly, "but I do not particularly like your way of getting wives."

Their visitors were not to remain above ten days with them. Luke had received his commission before he left London, and he was to rejoin the regiment at Brighton at the end of a fortnight.

No one but Mrs Bennet, regretted that their stay would be so short; and she made the most of the time, by outfitting her new daughter from her own wardrobe, and visiting about with her, and having very frequent parties at home. These parties were acceptable to all; to avoid a family circle was even more desirable to such as did think, than such as did not.

Betsy's affection for Luke, was just what John had expected to find it; and as he wrote to Edward, he did not think it equal to his for her. Their marriage had been brought about by the violence of his desires, rather than any wish of her's to be married;

and Edward replied that he suspected that Luke was not a young man to resist an opportunity of securing a life companion in such a way, having been introduced to vice by Wickham.

As for Luke; he was exceedingly fond of his new wife. She was his dear Betsy on every occasion; no one was to be put in competition with her for looks or agreeability. She did every thing best in the world; and one morning he came upon John sitting quietly with a book, and said, "I never gave you an account of my wedding, I believe. You were not by, when I told mamma, all about it. Are you not curious to hear how it was managed?"

"Not really," replied John, "I think there cannot be too little said on the subject."

"La! You are so strange!" said Luke, not heeding John's reply at all in his desire to boast about his wedding. "Well, and so we breakfasted at ten as usual; I thought it would never be over; for, by the bye, you are to understand, that my uncle and aunt were horrid unpleasant all the time we were with them. Even as we were dressing, I could hear my aunt, all the time to Betsy, preaching and talking away just as if she were reading a sermon; I don't believe Betsy heard a word of it, my aunt was in such a fuss! What's worse, if you'll believe me, we did not once put a foot out of doors, though we was there for a fortnight. Not one party, or scheme, or any thing. To be sure London was rather thin, but however the little Theatre was open. Well, and so just as the carriage came to the door, my uncle was called away upon business to that horrid man Mr Stone. And then, you know, when they get together, there is no end of it. Well, I was worried then that he would not return in time, for he was to give Betsy away, her father could not come from Brighton; and if we were beyond the hour, we could not be carried all day. But luckily, he came back again in ten minutes time, and then we all set out. However, I recollected afterwards, that if he had been prevented going, the wedding need not be put off, for Mr Darcy might have done as well."

"Mr Darcy!" repeated John, in utter amazement.

"Oh, yes! He insisted on coming, though I am sure no one wanted him there. But gracious me! I quite forgot! I ought not to have said a word about it. I promised them so faithfully! It was to be such a secret!"

"If it was to be secret," said John, "say not another word on the subject. You may depend upon my seeking no further, or asking you any questions."

"Thank you," said Luke, "for if you did, I would certainly tell you all, and then my uncle and Mr Darcy would be angry."

On such encouragement to ask, John was forced to put it out of his power, by leaving the room. He sat down immediately to write to Edward to tell him what he had learned from Luke, and to his aunt Gardiner with details of Luke and Betsy's visit to Longbourn.

Edward already knew that Mr Darcy was gone to London, and Miss Darcy was gone to stay at Rosings with her aunt. He knew not where the Bingleys and Hursts were gone. He also knew that it was business that took Mr Darcy to town, but even Miss Darcy did not know on what business he was gone and was unable to shed any light on the subject. Edward, back at home at Frithton Hall, wrote to Miss Darcy with the bare bones of the story; and offered to release her from their engagement, saying that his affections and wishes were unchanged, but one word from her would silence him on this subject for ever.

Her reply was full of surprise at Luke's sudden marriage, but as to their own marriage, though not as fluently expressed; her meaning was clear; she considered herself bound to him no matter what folly his brother may have committed, and she looked forward to her brother's return from London, when they would travel together to Pemberley, and arrangements for their own wedding could be made with Mr and Mrs Fellowes.

Reassured by the strength of her affection, and not being able to apply to Darcy himself for intelligence as to his business in London, Edward instead wrote to his aunt Gardiner, to request an explanation of what Luke had dropt to John; if it were compatible with the secrecy which had been intended.

"You may readily comprehend," he added, "what my curiosity must be to know how Mr Darcy should have been amongst you at such a time. Pray write instantly, and let me understand it – unless it is, for very cogent reasons, to remain in the secrecy which Luke seems to think necessary; and then I must endeavour to be satisfied with ignorance."

"Not that I shall, though," he added to himself, as he finished the letter, "and my dear aunt, if you do not tell me in an honourable manner, I shall certainly have to ask John or Miss Darcy to resort to tricks and stratagems to find it out."

John's delicate sense of honour would not allow him to seek any further information from any body after his letter to Edward, and so the matter rested, waiting for Mrs Gardiner's reply.

Chapter Thirty

Edward had the satisfaction of receiving an answer to his letter, as soon as he possibly could. He was no sooner in possession of it, than he hurried away to his own apartment, where he was least likely to be interrupted. He sat down in his dressing-room, and prepared to be enlightened; for the length of the letter convinced him that it did not contain a denial.

Gracechurch-street, Sept. 6

My dear nephew

I have just received your letter, and will devote this whole morning in answering it, as I foresee that a little writing will not comprise what I have to tell you. I must confess myself a little surprised at your application, knowing that you are on intimate terms with the Darcy family; your uncle is as surprised as I am – and nothing but the belief of your being a party concerned, would have allowed him to act as he has done. But if you are really innocent and ignorant, I must be more explicit. On the very day that we received word that your father was to come to London to seek Luke, Mr Darcy called here at Gracechurch-street, and was shut up with your uncle several hours. He came to tell Mr Gardiner that he had found where your brother and Mr Wickham were, and that he had seen and talked with them both. From what I can collect, he left Derbyshire the same day as you and Mr and Mrs Fellowes, and came to town with the resolution of hunting for them. The motive professed, was his conviction of its being owing to himself that Wickham's worthlessness had not been so well known, as to make it impossible for anyone to put themselves in his power, or follow his example. He generously imputed the whole to his mistaken pride, and confessed that he had before thought it beneath him, to lay his private actions open to the world. His character was to speak for itself. He called it, therefore, his duty to step forward, and endeavour to remedy an evil, which had been brought on by himself. I know not if he were thinking of Miss Darcy, and may be he had another motive; but if he had, it would not disgrace him. He had been some days in town, before he was able to discover them; but he had something to direct his search, which was more than your father or uncle had; and the consciousness of this, was another reason for his resolving to put right this situation. There is a lady, it seems, a Mrs Younge, who was some time ago governess to Miss Darcy, and was dismissed from her charge on some cause of disapprobation, though he did not say what. She then took a large house in Edward-street, and has since maintained herself by letting lodgings. This Mrs Younge was, he knew, intimately acquainted with Wickham; and he went to her for intelligence of him, as soon as he got to town. But it was two or three days before he could get from her what he wanted. She would not betray her trust, I suppose, without bribery and corruption, for she really did know where her friend was to be found. Wickham and Luke had indeed gone to her on their first arrival in London, and had she been able to receive them into her house, they would have taken up their abode with her. At length, however, our kind friend procured the wished-for direction.

They were in –street. He saw them both, and found them well-contented with their situation, and not at all concerned at the panic they had caused amongst their friends and family. Wickham confessed himself obliged to leave the regiment, on account of some debts of honour, which were very pressing; and scrupled not to lay all the ill-consequences of Luke's behaviour, on his own folly alone. He declared he knew nothing of Miss Cranshaw, and cared even less. He meant to resign his commission immediately; and as to his future situation, he could conjecture very little about it. He must go somewhere, but he did not know where, and he knew he should have nothing to live on. As for Luke, though his father were not imagined to be very rich, he would have been able to do something for Luke, and he agreed that Miss Cranshaw's situation must benefit from their early marriage.

They met several times, for there was much to be discussed. Wickham, of course, wanted more than he could get to take himself off to a far distant place, and trouble the Darcys no more; but at length both he and Luke were persuaded to be reasonable about their future prospects. Every thing being settled between them, Mr Darcy's next step was to make your uncle acquainted with it, and he first called in at Gracechurch-street the evening before their first meeting. But Mr Bennet was still with us until the following morning, when he returned to Longbourn at our request; and Mr Darcy did not judge your father to be a person whom he could so properly consult as your uncle. Therefore he readily postponed seeing Mr Gardiner till after the departure of your father. He did not leave his name, and till the next day, it was only known that a gentleman had called on business. On Saturday he came again. Your father was gone, your uncle was at home, and, as I said before, thcy had a great deal of talk together.

They met again on the Sunday, and then I saw him too. It was not all settled before Monday; as soon as it was, the express was sent off to Longbourn. But our visitor was very obstinate. I fancy, Eddie, that obstinacy may run in the family, and you will need to have a care with Miss Darcy! Nothing was to be done that he did not do himself; though I am sure (and I do not speak it to be thanked, therefore saying nothing about it,) your uncle would most readily have settled the whole. They battled it together for a long time, which was more than either gentleman concerned in it deserved. But at last your uncle was forced to yield, and instead of being allowed to be of use to his sister's family, was forced to put up with only having the probable credit of it, which went sorely against the grain; and I really believe your letter of this morning gave him great pleasure, because it required an explanation that would rob him of his borrowed feathers, and give the praise where it was due.

But, Eddie, this must go no further than yourself, or John at most. You know pretty well, I suppose, what has been done for both Mr Wickham and for Luke and Betsy. Mr Wickham's debts are to be paid, amounting, I believe to considerably more than a thousand pounds, and his commission purchased.

A thousand pounds has been settled on Betsy, and a commission purchased for Luke in a separate regiment. The reason why all this was to be done by him alone, was such as I have given above. It was owing to him, to his reserve, and want of proper consideration, that Wickham's character had been so misunderstood, and consequently that he had been received and noticed as he was. Perhaps there was some truth in this, though I doubt whether his reserve, or anybody's reserve, can be answerable for the event. But in spite of all this fine talking, my dear nephew, you may rest perfectly assured that your uncle would never have yielded, if we had not given Mr Darcy credit for wanting to ensure his sister's happiness. When all this was resolved on, he returned to his own town house, and agreed to be in London once more when the wedding too place, and all money matters were then to receive the last finish.

I believe I have now told you every thing. Luke came to us, and Miss Cranshaw was escorted here also; but I would not tell you how little I was satisfied by Luke's behaviour while he staid with us, if had not perceived by John's letter last Wednesday, that his coming home was exactly of a piece with it, and therefore what I tell you now, can give you no fresh pain. Miss Cranshaw was better behaved, although there was some grumbling amongst the servants at having to wait on her. I talked to her repeatedly in the most serious manner, representing to her the folly of her actions, and I attempted to talk to Luke as well about all the wickedness of what he had done, and all the unhappiness he had brought on his family, and Betsy's family. If either of them heard me, it was by good luck, for I am sure they did not listen. Mr Darcy was punctual with his return, and, as Luke informed John, attended the wedding. He dined with us the next day, and was to leave town again to collect his sister who was staying with his aunt and fiancé. I take this opportunity to say how much I like Mr Darcy, and how pleased I am that you have an understanding with his sister. I think he will be a very valuable brother to you. His understanding and opinions all please me; he wants nothing but a little more liveliness, and may be his marriage to Miss De Bourgh will teach him that. I have an invitation from him to visit Pemberley whenever I wish; Mr Gardiner is to go fishing with Mr Darcy, while I go all round the park in a low phaeton, with a nice little pair of ponies. But I must write no more. The children have been wanting me this half hour. Your's, very sincerely, M Gardiner.

The contents of this letter astonished Edward. The vague and unsettled suspicions which uncertainty had produced of what Mr Darcy might have been doing to forward her brother's marriage, which he had feared to encourage, as an exertion of goodness too great to be probable, and at the same time dreaded to be just, from the pain of obligation, were proved beyond their greatest extent to be true! He had gone purposefully to town, ensuring his sister's safety and removal from any where Wickham might be first, he had taken on himself all the trouble and mortification attendant on such a research; in which supplication had been necessary to a woman whom he must abominate and despise, and where he was reduced to meet, frequently meet, reason with, persuade, and finally bribe, the man whom he always most wished to avoid, and whose very name it was punishable for him to pronounce.

He had done all this for his sister; so that she might marry where her heart dictated, no matter what the circumstances of her husband's family. But now he would be a brother-in-law of a washerwoman! Every kind of pride must revolt from the connection. He had to be sure done very much.

Edward was ashamed to think how much Mr Darcy had done for his family. He had given a reason for his interference, which asked no extraordinary stretch of belief. It was reasonable that he should feel he had been wrong; he had liberality, and he had the means of exercising it; though Edward would place Miss Darcy's happiness as her brother's principal inducement, it was still painful, exceedingly painful, to know that the Bennet family were under obligations to a person who could never receive a return. They owed the restoration of Luke, his future profession, every thing to Mr Darcy.

He was roused from his reverie, by a manservant seeking him out, and requesting his presence in the study. He took down both letters and gave them into Mr Fellowes's hands to read for himself. His conclusions were the same; that Mr Darcy had acted to preserve the character and happiness of his sister, and to rid the Darcy family of a very troublesome hanger-on.

"But my dear son," he exclaimed in distress, "a washerwoman? What does Miss Darcy say? Will her brother call off your engagement? What will I tell Mrs Fellowes?"

Edward reassured him that, as far as he could tell, Miss Darcy was holding to the engagement, but that they were both waiting for Mr Darcy to bring her home to Pemberley again; and of her reference to their marriage following shortly after. He did not add that he believed she was not in possession of all the facts about Luke's hasty marriage, nor the sort of woman he was married to, and this did give him considerable discomposure of spirits.

Chapter Thirty-one

Mrs Luke Bennet was perfectly satisfied with her stay at her in-laws' house; with the attention she had received from them and all their neighbours, and with the new clothes which her mother-in-law had given her to mark her marriage. If she had been a young woman of any diffidence, she would have been over-awed by the size of Longbourn, and the stile in which the family lived; but she believed herself equal to any society, and, apart from commenting on the number of different rooms for different functions, she showed no signs of inferiority. The day of their departure soon came, and Mrs Bennet was forced to submit to a separation, which, as her husband by no means entered into her scheme of their all going to Brighton, was likely to continue at least a twelvemonth.

"Oh! My dear children," she cried, "when shall we meet again?"

"Oh, lord! I don't know. Not these two or three years perhaps."

"Write to me very often, my dear."

Betsy agreed, but in truth she did not know how to write, and all correspondence would have to be carried out by Luke, who was an indifferent correspondent at best. They made their adieus, and Betsy made Mr Bennet a pretty curtsey, which he returned with a stiff bow. The newly-wed couple stepped into the chaise, and were gone.

The loss of her son and daughter made Mrs Bennet very dull for several days.

"I often think," said she, "that there is nothing so bad as parting with one's friends. One seems so forlorn without them."

"That is the consequence you see, Madam, of marrying a son," said Mark, "it must make you satisfied that your other four are yet single."

"It is no such thing. Luke does not leave because he is married; but only because his regiment happens to be so far off. If that had been nearer, he would not have gone so soon. Perhaps the regiment may be quartered at Meryton again, how much joy would that give to us all!"

The next morning brought an entirely unexpected joy to Mr Bennet in the form of another letter from Mr Collins. It was most unexpected, for as far as Mr Bennet was aware, Mr Collins had nothing left to thank him for. He sent for John, and when he arrived in the library, gestured him over to a seat by the fire place, and they both sat down.

He then said, "I have received a letter from Mr Collins this morning, and knowing how much enjoyment you share with me in his communications, I thought you might like to hear it."

"From Mr Collins! And what can he have to say?"

"Oh! Nothing of any import, you may be sure, but what relates to your brother, Edward. I shall not sport with your intelligence by reading what he says at the start. This is what follows:

'Let me now add a short hint on another subject, of which we have been advertised by another authority; Lady Catherine de Bourgh herself. She, with her usual condescension, expressed what she felt on the occasion; when it became apparent, that on the score of some family objections on the part of the Bennet family, she would never give her consent to what she termed so disgraceful a match with her own niece. I thought it my duty to give the speediest intelligence of this to you, my dear Sir, that you may counsel your son to raise his eyes elsewhere, and not run hastily into a marriage which has not been properly sanctioned.'

"Are you aware of any attachment relating to your brother and Miss De Bourgh? I cannot think when they might have met."

"Edward?" asked John, "No, his attachment is not to Miss De Bourgh, but to Miss Darcy!"

"Indeed! But it is no longer my place to hear of such matters; your intelligence is more up to date than mine. I was not aware of Edward's knowing Miss Darcy, nor of their attachment. But to return to Mr Collins's letter; do you wish to hear the rest?"

"Oh! Yes. Pray read on."

"He moreover adds; 'I am truly rejoiced that your youngest son's sad business has been so well hushed up, and am only concerned that the extent of his depravity should be so generally known. I must not, however, neglect the duties of my station, or refrain from declaring my amazement, at hearing that you received the young couple into your house as soon as they were married. It was an encouragement of vice; and had I been the rector of Longbourn, I should very strenuously have opposed it. You ought certainly to forgive them as a Christian, but never to admit them in your sight, or allow their names to be mentioned in your hearing.'

"That is his notion of Christian forgiveness! The rest of his letter is only about his dear Charlotte's situation; but John, I fear you will have to warn your brother to call off his engagement to Miss Darcy. Now are you not diverted?"

"Oh!" cried John, "I am excessively diverted. But it is so strange. And I will warn Edward about Lady Catherine, but I would not tell him to call off his engagement for the world."

"It is indeed this strangeness that makes Mr Collins my best correspondent. I would not give up this connection for any consideration. For what do we live but to make sport for our neighbours, and laugh at them in our turn? Well, well, so Eddie has made an offer for Miss Darcy? It would be a most eligible match, but is he truly fond of her? And she of him?"

John was earnest and solemn in his assurances that Miss Darcy was really the object of Edward's choice, and enumerated with energy all her good qualities, as advertised by Edward in his letters; and Mr Bennet was satisfied.

"In that case," said he, "I have no more to say. If this be the case, then she is deserving of him; I would not wish to see him married to a woman he could not truly esteem."

Had Mr Bennet and John but known it; Lady Catherine had not contented herself with issuing a warning to the Bennet family through her mouthpiece, Mr Collins; she had also spoken directly to her niece, who was staying with her at Rosings. Miss Darcy had just confirmed to Edward her intention of continuing with her engagement, was at any moment expecting her brother to return from his business in London, and was taking a turn about Rosings Park, when she observed her aunt approaching.

"My dear," said Lady Catherine as she arrived at Miss Darcy's side, and took her arm, "let us walk into the wilderness."

Miss Darcy assented, and they walked on before Lady Catherine continued,

"Now, you cannot be at a loss to understand why I have sought you out away from the house. Your own heart, your own conscience must tell you why I come."

Miss Darcy looked with unaffected astonishment.

"Indeed, you are mistaken, aunt. I know you do not often take a turn about the park, and I am not at all able to account for the honour of your joining me here."

"Georgiana!" replied her ladyship, in an angry tone, "you ought to know, that I am not to be trifled with. But however sly you may choose to be, you shall not find me so. My character has ever been celebrated for its sincerity and frankness, and in a cause of such moment as this, I shall certainly not depart from it. A report of a most alarming nature reached me this morning. I was told that you, my niece, my own niece, was resolved on marriage to Mr Edward Bennet. Though I know it must be a scandalous falsehood; though I would not injure you so much as to suppose the truth of it possible, I instantly resolved on finding you out, that I might make my sentiments known to you."

"But aunt," said Georgiana, colouring with astonishment and some little fear, "if you believed it impossible to be true, I wonder you took the trouble to come to me and ask. What could you propose by it?"

"At once to insist on you confirming that such a report is completely untrue."

"Is there such a report in existence?"

"Indeed! It is being most industriously circulated by the Bennet family. How do you not know that such a report is spread abroad? Think of your brother! Think of your own credit and respectability!"

"If there is such a report, Madam, I shall be the last person to know of it. I have no contact with the Bennet family."

"Miss Darcy, do you know what you and your brother owe to me? I have not been accustomed to such sauce as this. I am almost the nearest relation you both have in the world, and I am entitled to know all your dearest concerns. This match, which the Bennets have the presumption to aspire to, can never take place."

Georgiana hesitated for a moment, and then said,

"I am by honour and inclination bound to Mr Edward Fellowes, Aunt, but he has not told the Bennet family of our attachment."

Lady Catherine was most displeased.

"Honour, decorum, prudence, nay interest, forbid this match! The upstart pretension of a young man without family, connections, or fortunes, to be married to my niece! If he were sensible of his own good, he would not wish to quit the sphere in which he was brought up."

"He is a gentleman's son, and I am a gentleman's daughter; so far we are equal."

"True. You are a gentleman's daughter, and he may well be a gentleman's son; I have some knowledge of his father. But his mother! And his uncles and aunts! Do not imagine me ignorant of their condition."

"Whatever his upbringing may have been, he is now the son of Mr and Mrs Fellowes, who are most respectable and wealthy people, known to my brother, and living in Frithton Court, adjacent to Pemberley. He stands to inherit a huge fortune and a large estate. Therefore, his connections can be nothing for you to worry about."

"Whatever he may have become; he is not worthy of becoming my nephew. Tell me once and for all, are you engaged to him?"

Though Miss Darcy would not, for the mere purpose of obliging her aunt, have answered this question; she could not but say, after a moment's deliberation,

"We have entered into an understanding, but have been waiting for my brother to finish his business in London, to forward the match."

"Georgiana! I am shocked and astonished that this should have been fixed up without my knowledge and consent. I expected you to have more sense of what is owed to your family."

Miss Darcy begged to return into the house, but Lady Catherine was not yet finished.

"Not so hasty, if you please. Let us sit down here. I have by no means done. To all the other objections I have already urged, I have still another to add. I am no stranger to the youngest Bennet boy's infamous behaviour at Brighton. I know it all. His marriage to a washerwoman, was a patched-up business at the expence of his uncle and father. And is such a woman to be my nephew's sister? Your sister? Anne's sister? Heaven and earth! Of what are you thinking? Are the shades of Pemberley to be thus polluted?"

"No more, aunt, please!" Georgiana cried, in some distress, "I must beg to return to the house."

And she spoke as she rose. Lady Catherine rose also and they turned back. Her ladyship was highly incensed.

"You have no regard, then, for the honour and credit of our family! Unfeeling, selfish girl! Do you not consider that this connection you propose must disgrace us all in the eyes of every body?"

"I have given my word, aunt." Was all that Georgiana could say in the face of this onslaught.

"You refuse, then, to oblige me. You refuse to obey the claims of duty, honour and gratitude. You are determined to ruin our family in the opinion of all our friends, and make us the contempt of the world."

"Neither duty, nor honour, nor gratitude," replied Georgiana, emboldened by the sight of her brother coming towards them across the lawn, "have any possible claim on me, in the present instance. No principle of either, would be violated by my marriage with Mr Edward Fellowes. And with regard to the resentment of my family, or the indignation of the world, if the former were excited by my marriage, it would not give me one moment's concern – and the world in general would have too much sense to join in the scorn."

Lady Catherine had also seen Mr Darcy approaching.

"And this is your real opinion! This is your final resolve! Very well. I shall know how to act. Do not imagine, Georgiana, that your brother will agree with this course of action you have chosen. I hoped to find you reasonable; but depend upon it, I will carry my point. I am most displeased with you. Return now into the house, and let me speak with Mr Darcy."

Georgiana dropt her a small curtsey, and hurried towards her brother, giving him a look of mute appeal, as she passed. She was feeling considerable uneasiness as to the possible consequences of Lady Catherine's interference, now that she was applying to her nephew; and Georgiana did not know how he would take her representation of the evils attached to a connection with the Bennet family. The arguments Lady Catherine had made, appeared weak and ridiculous to Georgiana, but she did not know whether her brother's notions of dignity would find them containing much good sense and solid reasoning, or not. She knew not what she should do if he were to forbid the match.

As she passed in to the house, her cousin Anne called out to tell her that Mr Darcy was come; but Georgiana hurried on past Anne's sitting room, to her own apartment, where she could sit alone and think. What had Lady Catherine been talking of? A washerwoman? Edward had mentioned a marriage – she hastily snatched up his last letter, scanning it with impatience for the details her aunt had mentioned. But beyond writing that his youngest brother was lately married, and due to return to Brighton to the militia, there were no further details. Georgiana was bewildered and knew not what to think. She did the only thing she could do; which was to pour out her heart on paper to Edward, and to warn him that, should her brother take her aunt's side; their marriage may have to be postponed, or might not take place at all.

Chapter Thirty-two

The spiritless condition that Mrs Bennet had been thrown into by the loss of her son and daughter, was shortly relieved and her mind opened up again to the agitation of hope, by an article of news which began to be in circulation. The housekeeper at Netherfield had received orders to prepare for the arrival of her master, who was coming down in a day or two, to shoot there for several weeks. Mrs Bennet was quite in the fidgets; for she had not quite given up on the hope of preferment for her sons at Mr Bingley's hands, even though Mr Bennet pointed out to her, that she was running out of sons for Mr Bingley to assist. However, if it were to be a shooting party, then the ladies might not be in residence, and so John could not be encouraged to pay his addresses to Miss Bingley; for Mrs Bennet did not know he had already been soundly rejected. But, considering the matter from every side, there was also the benefit to John in maintaining a friendship with Mr Bingley, as a neighbouring land-owner, and so Mrs Bennet smiled at her sister Philips who first brought her the news, and then shook her head by turns.

"Well, well, and so Mr Bingley is coming down. Well, so much the better. Not that I care about it though. He is of no further use to us, you know, and I am sure I never want to see him again. But, however, he is very welcome to come to Netherfield if he likes it. And who knows what may happen? But that is nothing to us. You know, we agreed long ago never to mention a word about it. And so, is it quite certain that he is coming?"

"You may depend upon it," replied her sister, "for Mrs Nicholls was in Meryton last night; I saw her passing by, and went out myself on purpose to know the truth of it; and she told me that it was certain true. He comes down on Thursday at the latest, very likely on Wednesday. She was going to the butcher's, she told me, on purpose to order in some meat on Wednesday, and she has got three couple of ducks, just fit to be killed."

"It is hard," opined Charles, "that this poor man cannot come to a house, which he has legally hired, without raising all this speculation! We must leave him to himself, and if he wishes to renew our acquaintance, let him seek us out. He knows where we live. It is not seemly to be running after our neighbours every time they go away, and come back again."

Mrs Bennet and Mrs Philips were rather astonished by this speech from Charles, who had turned very serious now that Luke and the militia were gone, and his future had been taken in hand by his father. He had started studying serious works with Mark in the evenings, and applied himself to his tutors with an exertion that was most admirable in one who had never been hard-working before. His speech had the effect of ending the conference between his mother and his aunt, and his aunt shortly afterwards went home again to see if there were any more intelligence to be gleaned from the streets and shops of Meryton. His mother began at once to plan a dinner for Mrs Long, and the Gouldings, to which Mr Bingley, and his unknown household, would all be invited.

And so the subject which had been so warmly canvassed between Mr and Mrs Bennet, about a twelvemonth ago, was now brought forward again.

"As soon as ever Mr Bingley comes, my dear," said Mrs Bennet, "you will wait on him, of course."

"No, no. You forced me into visiting him last year, and promised if I went to see him, he should marry his sister to one of our sons, and provide places for all the rest. But it ended in nothing, and I will not be sent on a fool's errand again."

Mrs Bennet endeavoured to represent to him how absolutely necessary such an attention would be from all the neighbouring gentlemen, on his return, but Mr Bennet was adamant that no such visit would be paid this time.

Had Mrs Bennet but known it, her peace of mind was to be disturbed again very shortly, and from a most unexpected source. John decided it was time to speak to Maria, and if she were willing to consent to an engagement, to take his offer to Sir William Lucas. If Maria or the Lucases did not wish to be associated by marriage with the Bennets; now was the time to find that out. He went first to his father, for his marrying would materially affect the whole family, and he would not take such a step without his father's knowledge and blessing.

"Well, John," said his father, when the matter was laid before him. "This will be a change indeed for the household; is your mother aware of your intentions?"

"Not yet, Sir," replied John, "I thought it best to come to you first."

"And Maria Lucas is your choice."

"Yes, Sir."

"She is a sensible girl, to be sure; as Lady Catherine would observe, an active, useful sort of person, not brought up high, but able to make a small income go a good way. You know, of course, that I cannot do much for you on your marriage after your youngest brother's performance; and there is your brother

Charles to put through University; we may need to buy him a preferment, if we cannot find any body with influence, or a living to bestow."

"I understand, Sir," John said, "it will take us time to retrench, but I still wish to marry as soon as possible; I have every confidence that Maria will be of great assistance in restoring the family, and will not require luxuries. I believe she has some little fortune from her father as Charlotte took none with her on her marriage to Mr Collins."

"That's as may be," said Mr Bennet, "but it is a comfort to think, that whatever befalls this family, you have an affectionate mother who will always make the most of it. Well, well, to think how much your mother has always wanted a daughter and now she will have three all at once! I shall be very fond of all my daughters-in-law, to be sure; Betsy is perhaps my favourite, but I think I shall like yours and Edward's wives quite as well."

Despite the worry of how his mother would react to a second daughter-in-law, and more over one who would be living in the house she would go on to be mistress of; John walked over to Lucas Lodge. It was all speedily settled between Maria and himself, as neither was in the habit of making long speeches; and they went to Sir William and Lady Lucas together, as Maria assured John of her parents' immediate compliance with their wishes.

Their complete agreement was, indeed, bestowed with the same joyful alacrity with which they accepted Mr Collins as a son-in-law. This was another most eligible match for a daughter, to whom this time, they could give a little fortune. Charlotte had indeed taken none with her to Mr Collins, and her small share could be bestowed upon Maria, and added to her own. Lady Lucas waited until the happy couple were taking a turn about the grounds of Lucas Lodge, before beginning to calculate with more interest than the matter had ever excited before, how many years longer Mr Bennet was likely to live; and

Sir William gave it as his decided opinion, that whenever John should be in possession of the Longbourn estate, it would be highly expedient that both he and his wife should make their appearance at St James's. It was indeed the most unlooked for relief to Maria's loving parents: to have two daughters well married, was a blessing indeed, and her younger sisters could form hopes of coming out a year or two sooner than they might otherwise have done.

Maria's marriage would be very different to her sister's; there was a strong foundation of intimacy and affection upon which to base their future together; for though Maria knew as well as Charlotte that marriage was the only honourable provision for herself, as a well-educated young woman of small fortune, she was also comfortably aware that she was much more fortunate than her sister, in obtaining a husband she could truly esteem.

John walked home again to inform his family of the successful outcome of his application. His mother, all unawares, was sitting alone in the breakfast room; Mr Bennet was in his library, Charles was studying with his tutor, and Mark was at work with his uncle Philips.

With a little gentle preparation, John told his mother that he was to marry Maria Lucas, as soon as a licence could be arranged. She was too much overpowered to say a great deal at first; but her feelings sound found a rapid vent, and she hurried instantly to her husband, calling out as she entered the library,

"Oh! Mr Bennet, you are wanted immediately; I am all in an uproar. You must come and tell John he must not marry Maria Lucas; make him understand this is not at all the thing! We were agreed that he must marry Miss Bingley, for she has a fortune, while Maria Lucas can have nothing at all."

John followed his mother into the study in time to hear his father reply,

"John is of age, and will be of means one day. I see no reason to prevent this marriage. Now, my dear," to his wife, "I have two small favours to request. First, that you will allow me the free use of my understanding on the present occasion; I have not agreed that John shall marry Miss Bingley at any time. Secondly, I shall be glad to have the library to myself as soon as may be."

Not yet, however, in spite of her disappointment in her husband, did Mrs Bennet give up her point. She talked to John again and again, coaxed and threatened by turns. John with all possible mildness kept to his determination, and endeavoured to bring her to an acceptance of his marriage. Mrs Bennet continued, with an echo of Charles's former peevishness,

"I have no pleasure in talking to undutiful children. Not that I have much pleasure indeed in talking to any body. People who suffer as I do from nervous complaints can have no great inclination for talking. Nobody can tell what I suffer! But it is always so. Those who do not complain are never pitied."

John held his ground, but Mrs Bennet was really in a most pitiable state. The very mention of any thing concerning the match threw her into an agony of ill humour, and wherever she went she was sure of hearing it talked of, for Sir William and Lady Lucas were quick to spread the good tidings all around their friends and acquaintances in Meryton and beyond.

The sight of Maria was odious to Mrs Bennet. As her successor in that house, she regarded her with jealous abhorrence. Whenever Maria came to see John, she concluded her to be anticipating the hour of possession; and whenever she spoke in a low voice to John, was convinced that they were talking of the Longbourn estate, and resolving to turn her out of the house, as soon as Mr Bennet was dead.

She complained bitterly of all this to her husband.

"Indeed, Mr Bennet," said she, "it is very hard to think that Maria Lucas should ever be mistress of this house, that I should be forced to make way for her, and live to see her take my place in it!"

"My dear, do not give way to such gloomy thoughts. Let us hope for better things. Let us flatter ourselves that I may be the survivor."

This was not very consoling to Mrs Bennet, and therefore, instead of making any answer, she went on as before.

"I cannot bear to think that she should have all of this estate. If it was not for the entail I should not mind it."

"What should you not mind?"

"I should not mind any thing at all."

"Let us be thankful that you are preserved from such a state of insensibility."

"I can never be thankful, Mr Bennet, for any thing about the entail. How any one could have the conscience to arrange it so that my house passes to a woman who is not even a family member, I cannot understand. Why should she have it more than any body else?"

"I leave it to yourself to determine," said Mr Bennet. However, it was very clear to him that it would be impolitic to bring Maria into the house upon her marriage to John, and so he arranged for a cottage on the estate to be prepared to receive the newlyweds, as his wedding gift to them.

John's marriage to Maria took place shortly after this conversation, and Mrs Bennet was so far resigned as to think it as inevitable as Charlotte's to Mr Collins; and even said once that she "wished they might be happy." The wedding took place, the bride and bridegroom took possession of Longbourn Cottage; and every body had as much to say or to hear on the subject as usual. John wrote to Edward of his happiness, and Edward replied that such a happy event could now teach the admiring multitudes of Meryton what connubial felicity really was; and what was more to the point, that he was about to discover his own fate, now that the Darcys were come back from Rosings.

Chapter Thirty-four

Happy for all her late-flowering maternal feelings was the day on which Mrs Fellowes's son, Edward, married their neighbour, Miss Darcy. Less happy was the same day for Lady Catherine De Bourgh, who had been unable to prevent her niece from marrying, and whose own daughter had run away to her cousin, and married to him on the same day. As Lady Catherine had previously consented to the marriage, and all the documents had already been drawn up, witnessed and signed, there was no other way of showing her disapprobation of her nephew's consent to her niece's marriage, than by staying away from his wedding.

Mrs Bennet was less affected by Edward's marriage, although she liked to talk of Mr and Mrs Fellowes, Miss Darcy and Mr Edward Bennet that was: her attention was more taken up with her grand-child; John and Maria's son, named after both his grandfathers. Mrs Bennet believed that this boy would one day be the master of Longbourn and that she would not have to give way to Maria Lucas after all. I wish I could say, for the sake of her family, that the accomplishment of her earnest desire in the settled establishment of all her sons, produced so happy an effect to make her a sensible, amiable, well-informed woman for the rest of her life; though perhaps it was lucky for her husband, who might not have relished domestic felicity in so unusual a form, that she still was occasionally nervous, and invariably silly.

Mr Bingley remained at Netherfield only for a twelvemonth, prompting Mrs Bennet to attempt to persuade her husband to buy it of Mr Morris, for her youngest son and daughter; once the restoration of peace dismissed them to a home. Mr Bennet sported with her on this hope, never actually uttering a negative, so that all her plans were kept alive, until Mr Morris unexpectedly married, and moved his new family into his own Hall.

Luke's letter to John on his marriage, was evidence that such an income as theirs, under the direction of two persons so extravagant in their wants, and so heedless of the future, must be very insufficient to their support.

The letter from Luke was to this effect:

"My dear John, I wish you joy. If you love Maria Lucas half as well as I do my dear Betsy, you must be very happy. It is a great comfort to have you and Edward so rich, and when you have nothing else to do, I hope you will think of us. I am sure I would like a place at court very much, and I do not think we shall have quite money enough to live upon without some help. Any place would do, of about three or four hundred a year; but, however, do not speak to Edward about it, if you had rather not. Your's, &tc."

As Luke certainly intended; John passed the letter on to Edward, who offered such relief as it was in his power to afford, but who enjoined John to attempt to put an end to every intreaty and expectation outlined in the letter, in his reply. Despite that, whenever the couple changed their quarters, either John or Edward was sure of being applied to, for some little assistance towards discharging their bills.

Their life was unsettled in the extreme; they were always moving from place to place in quest of a cheap situation, and always spending more than they ought. Her affection for him soon sunk into indifference, his lasted a little longer, and despite her attempts at becoming a lady, poor Betsy retained all the claims to reputation which her marriage had given her.

Frithton Court was, for now, Georgiana's home, and it was in such easy distance of Pemberley, that the two households were almost living as one, and every body's mutual attachment was exactly what Edward had hoped to see. Anne flourished in this atmosphere, and to Georgiana's astonishment, became lively, and sportive in her manners and conversation, especially to her husband. Mr Darcy had always inspired in his sister a respect which almost overcame her affection, but his response to his wife's open pleasantry, demonstrated to Miss Darcy just how much he had changed on his marriage, and how wrong she had been to fear his temper.

Lady Catherine was extremely indignant on the marriages of her daughter, niece and nephew; and as she gave way to all the genuine frankness of her character, in her reply to Darcy's letter which announced all the arrangements, she sent him language so very abusive, especially of Edward, that for some time all intercourse was at an end. But at length, by his sister's persuasion, Darcy was prevailed on to overlook the offence, and seek a reconciliation, for his wife's sake as much as his own. After a little further resistance on the part of his aunt, her resentment gave way, either to her affection for her daughter, or her curiosity to see how the Fellowes conducted themselves; and she condescended to wait upon them all at Pemberley, in spite of that pollution which its woods had received, not only from the frequent presence of Mr Edward Bennet Fellowes, but the visits of his aunt and uncle from the city.

With the Gardiners, all three couples were always on the most intimate terms. Mr and Mrs Fellowes, Darcy, his wife, and sister, really loved them as well as Edward could have hoped; and they were frequent visitors to both households.

Mr Wickham was never heard of again by any of his former acquaintance; but we may suppose that he too was dismissed to a house at the outbreak of peace, and eventually found his way back to Mrs Younge in London.

Mr and Mrs Darcy's marriage was happy; but childless, and thus three estates would, in time, be inherited by Mrs Bennet's grandchildren by her second son; a fact, which once explained to her, caused her much satisfaction indeed. Mark entered into an understanding with one of Mrs Goulding's daughters, and took over his uncle's practice on that worthy man's retirement. Charles attended Oxford, took his degree, and was assisted to a living at Pemberley by Mr Darcy, where he did indeed enjoy making sermons, as well as baptising, marrying and burying his parishioners as required, every bit as solemnly as Mr Collins at Hunsford. As for Mr and Miss Bingley; he chose not to marry, and his sister stayed with him to act as his housekeeper; both were also frequent visitors at Pemberley, until the darling wish of his sisters was then gratified and he bought an estate in a neighbouring county to Derbyshire; and thus they were all within thirty miles of each other.

APPENDIX - Recommended reading:

Roy and Lesley Adkins, 'Eavesdropping on Jane Austen's England', Hachette Digital, 2013

Jane Austen; all of her novels, including 'Lady Susan'. Best of luck with the sheer volume of attempts to continue 'Sanditon'; most of them are indescribably dire. I hesitantly recommend the recent ITV adaptation, and accompanying book.

Anna Dean, The Dido Kent Series, 2008 -2012; purchased by me as ebooks, but I'm sure they're available in hard copy as well.

Janice Hadlow, 'The Other Bennet Sister,' Macmillan, 2020

Georgette Heyer's novels; I know that other readers recommend Heyer, but I've never really got on with her style of writing.

Gill Hornby, 'Miss Austen', Century, 2020

Rory Muir, "Gentlemen of Uncertain Fortune, How Younger Sons Made Their Way in Jane Austen's England", (2019, Yale University Press)

John Mullan, 'What matters in Jane Austen', Bloomsbury, 2012 purchased by me as an ebook as well.

Jodi Taylor, 'A Bachelor Establishment,' 2015, purchased by me as an ebook.

John Wiltshire, 'The Hidden Jane Austen', Cambridge University Press, 2014

Lucy Worsley, 'Courtiers', faber and faber, 2010

Lighter reads set in Regency England:

Kathleen Baldwin – a series called 'My Notorious Aunt', 2004 – 2005, purchased by me as ebooks.

M C Beaton – she has written a huge quantity of novels set in Regency England – for lightweight, guilty pleasure, these are very readable.

D L Carter, 'Ridiculous', Corvallis Press, 2012

ABOUT THE AUTHOR

Gretel Hallett

I have been a fan of Jane Austen for many more years than I care to recall, and from time to time immerse myself once more in her incomparable world. I have also attempted several times to write prequels or sequels to her novels; this is the first Alternative Austen I have completed,  and only because I stole most of it from Austen herself. However, it has encouraged me to dig the others out of cold storage, and have a(nother) go at finishing them.

Printed in Great Britain
by Amazon

42284857R00116